CHAPTER 1

TALL MAN IN TOWN

A new street with a new name carried Gene Bannerman into Hondo City. Last time he'd been through here the steel tracks of the South-west Texas Line hadn't reached as far as Junction Crossing, fifty miles east; now it had touched newly named Hondo City before racing on west for Barranca and beyond, leaving something new called progress in its sooty wake.

The town may have changed plenty in that time but still looked none too good to the eyes of the tall man astride the powerful black. New clapboards and crib houses and jerry built structures masquerading as saloons didn't represent progress to him. But then he was different from most, as noisy, lamplit Hondo City was about to find out.

He crossed a heavy new plank bridge which

extended the avenue into the town's bustling heart
and took him to the long hitch rail, the bright lights
and the tin-pianny music of Rogan's Bar.

He stepped down, tied up and crossed the porch
to push the batwings open, standing there holding
them that way as his gaze swept the room which
slowly began to quieten as they grew aware that
'somebody different' had come amongst them.

For he was tall and somberly handsome in expensive grey suiting with a double gunrig buckled across
narrow hips, deep blue eyes seeming to take in everything at a glance as he stood there with the night
forming a black frame around him.

They thought he could be a lawman, high-roller,
man of the gun or perhaps some kind of businessman of the younger, tougher breed.

Only Rogan, cow-licked, portly and red-eyed
behind his bar knew exactly who he was, and
the rugged saloonkeeper was nervous, exactly the
way he had been when Gene Bannerman last came
to town with bunch of men he called Friends, with a
capital F.

'Gene Bannerman!' he called in greeting. 'Er,
great to see you back again, sir. The usual?'

The silence deepened. Many recognized the name
Gene Bannerman, knew it wasn't one to be taken
lightly.

Bannerman let go of the louvred doors and left
them flapping to silence behind his broad back as he
walked slowly into the centre of the bar-room, scan-
ning every face with a slow, deliberate stare. They
could now see the light film of dust coating steel grey

Two for Sonora

Big Gene Bannerman was a man with many friends, yet he always worked best alone when danger was part of the deal.

His journey to Mexico to save his sister's child had danger stamped all over it and when Bannerman swam his horse across the Rio Grande for Sonora, he had company. Bad company in the shape of Joe Delta, a mysterious man of the gun whom Bannerman didn't trust, but could not leave behind.

Locked in mortal combat with powerful Don Diego Rivera, his treacherous sons and more gringo gunmen than he'd ever seen in his native Texas, iron man Bannerman found his life on the line a dozen times as he challenged all the odds to rescue his sister's child from the clutches of the Don.

With the odds high and the death toll climbing in bloody Sonora, Bannerman, the man with the mission, vowed he would save the kid – even if his trail pard turned out to be a Judas in disguise who could so easily cost him his life.

By the same author

The Immortal Marshal

Two for Sonora

Ryan Bodie

A Black Horse Western

ROBERT HALE · LONDON

© Ryan Bodie 2004
First published in Great Britain 2004

ISBN 0 7090 7502 2

Robert Hale Limited
Clerkenwell House
Clerkenwell Green
London EC1R 0HT

Typeset by
Derek Doyle & Associates, Liverpool.
Printed and bound in Great Britain by
Antony Rowe Limited, Wiltshire

suiting and low-crowned black hat, dulling spurred boots. This man looked as though he had travelled a far piece even though there was no hint of weariness about him.

'I'm looking for a man,' Bannerman announced after a long pause. His chin lifted. 'A scum of a man in fact, a woman-molester and shootist by the name of Joe Delta.'

He waited for reaction. There was none. Blank faces and shrugging shoulders greeted him on all sides. Disappointment tugged at the corners of his mouth now, for he had dogged Delta a hundred miles and more and from the outset of his one-man hunt of the man who had gunned down an unarmed citizen up in Reno Wells. The sign had led him directly to Hondo City. Delta was hardly the kind of man to pass unnoticed wherever he might show up, so how come he had not yet been sighted here?

He turned to the bar. 'Do you know this man, Mr Rogan?'

'Sorry, can't help you, sir.'

Drinkers, percenters, blue-shirted railroad labour and tinhorn gamblers all stared at this. Rugged and overbearing Chev Rogan 'sirring' a man? Surely this had to be a first? The crowded room found itself taking a second and third look at the stranger named Bannerman, with drinkers and losers and two-dollar whores searching their memory files for what they knew about the man behind the name.

That it was a name of weighty significance there was no doubt. Most knew he hailed from the Keylock region, where he was purported to be both wealthy and powerful. Yet they had imaged Gene Bannerman to be a much older man, perhaps a large, grouchy old cattle baron attended by a bunch of flunkies. This image simply did not gell with that double gunrig and that clean-cut hardness of feature of someone whom even Rogan addressed as sir.

'Er, I'm sure he don't come from hereabouts, Mr Bannerman,' Rogan felt obliged to add as the silence dragged on. 'A gunny, you say?'

'A dog who interfered with a woman then shot down her unarmed husband when he objected – that is what I say, Mr Rogan,' Bannerman snapped. Another pause as his gaze swept the room. 'Six feet two, curly black hair, two six guns, dark rig and rides a paint horse. Anybody?'

No response.

He drew a ten-spot from a slash pocket of the tailored grey waistcoat and held it between two fingers. 'Are we sure about that?'

The lush in the hand-me-down garb and sorry top hat had his price, and it was a damn sight less than ten bucks.

'Crib Street two hours back, mister,' he croaked, coming forward with hand extended. 'I recall the tall feller and the paint hoss. Both looked plum tuckered. Gimme.'

Bannerman drew the note back from the reaching fingers.

'If you're lying you'll regret it,' he warned.

The drunk squinted in the bright lights.

'Black shirt and pants and a yeller hat,' he added.

'Spend it wisely, friend,' Bannerman replied, and

tucking the note into the grimed fist strode out without another word, leaving an audible sigh of relief in his wake.

But he wasn't always like this, this man from the north. Indeed most times and in most company Bannerman was genial and generous company, a man to ride the river with. Most times. But this was not one of them. Three days earlier a weeping Reno Wells woman with her husband and breadwinner fighting for his life from a bullet drilled into him by some flashy stranger 'just passing through', had arrived at the Bannerman mansion in Keylock with the information that the man responsible for the crime, one Joe Delta, had escaped lawful custody and was last seen hightailing south on a stolen horse, leaving a sheriff with a cracked skull in his dust.

There was no pursuit.

The woman came to him in the hope he might help her get some justice. She'd come to the right man. He was in his saddle within the hour, and now one hundred miles later was back astride the big barrelled black horse with white face and stockings, turning his back on the gleaming new railroad buildings to make his way to a new and sorry street in Railroad City, which was anything but gleaming; was nothing but ugly and all too familiar.

There was a Crib Street or its equivalent to be found in virtually every city, tank town or waterhole visited by the new wonder of the age, the railroad. The railroad brought new people with new money and the Crib Streets provided the pimps and prostitutes to cater for them.

A slim figure leaning against the doorframe of one of these tiny hut-houses called an invitation to him in the gloom but he did not spare the slattern a glance. Ahead the crooked street seemed to drift beneath a haze of railroad smoke and river mist, lightened here and there by the odd dim streetlight. Slow-moving figures moved through the haze like ghosts, and his lip curled, not in condemnation but in resentment that the West, his West, could be reduced to this all in the name of progress.

A man stepped from an alley and Bannerman's right hand flew to gunbutt. But it was just some bum with a humped back and a limp, not a fancy-dan two-gunner with a guilty conscience and his face on the truebills of Texas.

Times like this Bannerman never questioned the peculiarity of what he was doing, as others might see it. There was an extensive legal system in southern Texas to handle this sort of work. Yet here he was, a wealthy man a hundred miles from home sporting twin .45s and searching a red light section for a dangerous hellion.

Strange? Downright peculiar? Not when you happened to be Gene Bannerman it wasn't. He did not think like other men for the simple reason that he was different.

A door stood open. He paused. A man and a woman, bathed in oily yellow light, were embracing. He started at a sudden sound, whirled to see a kid of nine or ten shuffling by with an armful of towels.

His nose crinkled. The quicker he came face to

face with his man and got the hell out of here the better he would like it.

He strode on at a faster pace, eyes flicking from crib to alley to passing figures. Somewhere a doleful harmonica wailed, somewhere a woman sobbed wearily and hopelessly.

He was turning to gaze in the direction of the sound of the weeping when it happened. Dimly visible in the smoke-hazed maw of a fetid alley like a sunken sun, a blob of yellow. A hat. Next instant gunflame blossomed like a flower of death directly beneath the hat and Bannerman was diving and drawing in one fluent motion as the racketing roar of a revolver ripped the night apart.

Bullets were zipping above him as he hit the street on one shoulder and began fanning gun hammer. He drove in four rapid-fire rounds before holding. He heard the pound of receding steps coming back at him from the alley. In an instant he was on his feet and giving chase. Hitting the mouth of the tight little laneway, he glimpsed a lean shape ducking from sight at the far end. He covered the alley's length in a dozen giant strides, skidding the last ten feet to the corner, then dropped low again as six guns beat heavy thunder from somewhere off to his right.

From ground level, rolling on to his back, he snaked his right gun arm round the corner clapboards and triggered at the billowing gunflashes. He heard a bullet sing off something metallic, followed by a wild curse. The fast-fading shimmer of his last shot revealed a lean figure bending to retrieve something from the ground. A gun? He was ready to bet on it.

'Freeze, you bastard, or I'll shoot you dead!' he shouted.

There was a curse, a grunt of effort and his man was vaulting a low fence and taking off again.

Bannerman whipped out his second Colt and gave chase. He'd been ready to kill, but if he could take Delta alive, so much the better. Drag him back to Keylock and have belated justice both done and seen to be done in the eyes of the whole county, thereby exacting some value out of a low-life who otherwise plainly had no value at all.

Joe Delta – and he was now certain it was he – had a long head start along the gloomy back street but seemed to be favouring one leg.

Bannerman raised his cutter and put a round over the runner's head. But he kept on, suddenly cutting sideways into a side street, and was gone again. When Bannerman reached the corner to peer around it, the street was empty.

Nothing but closed doors and lights showing dully from behind drawn curtains. This was the crooked and twisted section of rambling Crib Street, he realized. With every sense intensely alert he strode to and fro until suddenly the lights in a crib with a scarred green door blinked out.

Might not be be anything, but then again. . . .

He hit the door with his shoulder and a lock burst, spattering screws and timber slivers into the interior darkness. He dived low as he came in, rolling to one side and roaring at the top of his lungs, 'Everyone freeze or I'll cut loose!' adding emphasis to the words by driving a slug into the low ceiling before rolling aside once again.

Something hard and vicious slammed into the floor where he'd just been sprawled. Then a woman's cry: 'For God's sake surrender, Joe, you haven't got a chance!' Then, 'Whoever you are, don't shoot, he hasn't got a gun!'

'Delta,' Bannerman barked, 'walk to the doorway and stand there where I can see you. I mean now.'

'Who the hell are y—?'

'Just do it or you are a dead man.'

There was a moment's pulsing silence followed by the slow drag of feet, laboured breathing. A tall silhouette appeared in the doorway and Bannerman came up to one knee, six gun cocked and ready.

'You, the woman. Make a light and be fast about it.'

He was aware he was breathing hard as he knelt there listening to the woman's rustling movements in the blackness. Outside all had fallen quiet as if Crib Street was holding its breath. He heard the rattle of matches before the flare of light filled the room, revealing the scantily dressed figure of the woman lifting the lamp glass at the table. The tall figure in the doorway glared at him with total hatred, hands at shoulder level, weight on one foot.

Bannerman rose slowly as light filled the room. The gunman's face suppurated with fury.

'I knew it was you,' he snarled. 'I saw you at the canyon, and again forty miles farther north, at Jubal Creek crossing. What are you – law?'

'Move where I can see you,' Bannerman ordered the woman with a gesture, not taking his eyes off his

13

catch. He stepped up to him, flipped the empty Colt from the man's holster then dragged him deeper into the room and swiftly bound him. 'No, I'm just a citizen, Delta, but one you won't forget when—'

'Gene!'

The woman's sudden cry brought him whirling about to see her clearly for the first time. She stood by the bureau with one hand to her face, a slender, strikingly beautiful woman in her thirties with raven hair tumbling to her shoulders and dark eyes wide with shock and disbelief.

'Jordan?' he croaked, scarcely believing his eyes as he gaped at the sister he had neither seen or heard of in ten long years.

'Hey, Jordy,' complained hogtied Joe Delta, the ropes chafing his bound wrists as he wriggled in his chair. 'Will you cut the jawbone for a second and give a man a drink before he croaks from thirst, goddamnit.'

'You'll live,' Bannerman snapped, taking out a chased silver cigar case from an inside pocket of his silk-lined jacket. He set a cheroot between his teeth and did not take his eyes from his sister's face as he patted his pockets for his pocket flint. 'My God, Jordan, how in hell did you—'

'No, don't start,' his sister warned, now seated defensively across the table from him, fingers interlaced on the oilcloth, hair and eyes as black as night against the pallor of her skin. 'Do you realize I had hoped to live the rest of my life without having to listen to one of your sanctimonious sermons again, brother dear?'

'So, what is this anyway?' grinned Delta, sensing the enmity and enjoying it, a man with little to enjoy at the moment. 'And how come you've never got to tell me you had a brother, baby? And not just any old common or garden brother either, let me tell you. No siree. Up Keylock way, why, Mr Gene Bannerman is like the law, the moneybags and the goddamn patron saint all rolled into one – ain't that so, Mr Big?'

'If you want me to gag you I can arrange it,' Bannerman warned. There was no force in his words however. Right then he was stunned, appalled, hurting. Having long since given up his only sibling for dead, it was both exhilarating to discover her still alive and yet he was horrified by her circumstances. He was looking at someone who once had been belle of every ball, the queen of Fulton County and quite probably the loveliest girl he'd ever seen, now a grown woman selling her body on a sleazy back street in a stinking railroad town and associating with outlaws and gunmen.

But still your sister, whispered an inner voice, and he made himself bite back the words that came unbidden to his lips. A combination of luck and coincidence had led him here to Crib Street; he must not allow what his sister might call his 'Camelot side' to intrude on this moment and further threaten their thus far fragile and uncertain reunion.

He said gently, 'Jordan, what happened to you? You just disappeared after our folks passed away. I didn't stop searching for you for two years. Why?'

'Does it really matter now?'

'It matters to me.' Bannerman studied his sister

15

keenly. They had been close once but were inexorably drifting apart at the time of their parents' death, an event made worse by her already heavy drinking culminating in her eventual disappearance from Fulton County. 'You had better tell me, sister. Did your disappearance have anything to do with me?'

'Everything.'

Gene stiffened. 'Explain.'

'Yeah, you had better explain, Jordy,' Delta put in. 'I never met this geezer before but I can tell he doesn't like what he's hearing or seeing one little bit. I heard folks say in Keylock that your big brother reckons he's just about picture perfect and the highest quality Texican to be found between the Red and the Rio, so you'd better break your news to him carefully on account he might bruise easy, honey babe.'

Bannerman ignored him. He was focused only upon whatever his sister might have to say.

And suddenly she had a great deal to say, scarce any of it welcome to his ears.

'All right, Gene,' she sighed, pouring herself a shot from a bottle without a label, 'if you insist.' She took a slug and didn't even cough. 'I simply grew tired of living in the shadow of someone who thought himself so wonderful, and who considered his sister as something far, far short of that level. You were always the best scholar, athlete, business brain, hunter, dancer . . . name it and you excelled at it, as mother and father constantly reminded me. You never grew tired of lecturing me and pointing out how I could be better, and when you were so hard on

16

me when I began drinking, that was just the last straw. I simply walked away from you, Gene, and I can honestly say I've never regretted it. So if you wanted the truth, now you have it.'

'This gets better and better,' enthused Delta. 'So tell me, Jordy, all this time I've known you, did you realize older brother was Mr Big up in Keylock County?'

'Only over the past couple of years since he got famous,' Jordan said with a bitter twist on that final word. She drained her glass. 'Gene Bannerman, cattle king. Friend of the poor and defender of the weak. The winner on all fronts and the light in the morning sky.' Her red mouth twisted. 'So, what does it feel like to be so wonderful and then discover your kid sister charges two dollars a trick on skid row, Lancelot?'

Bannerman had not been called that name in over a decade, ever since in fact he lost touch with his sister. The reference to his youthful fascination with Arthurian legend and the age of chivalry was not intended as a compliment but rather as a perjorative. It hurt. But then so did everything else in this ugly railroad town, in this liquor-scented room, this stinking night.

With a sigh he turned his attention to his prisoner. 'Where do you fit in here? Just another paying customer?'

'Old, old friends,' came the response. 'Isn't that so, honey? Yes, we go back quite a ways and have crossed plenty of rivers together. We're alike, you see. Neither of us likes stuffed shirts or true-blue heroes.

We like to live fast, have fun and the hell with the consequences. Right Jordy?'

'Joe is the only true friend I have,' Jordan stated.

'In that case you are in even more trouble than I thought,' Gene said acidly. 'Did he happen to tell you he attacked a woman and shot a man in Keylock? I'm taking him back to set him before a judge.'

'Still playing God, I see, brother? Nothing has changed, has it?'

'I guess it hasn't at that.' Bannerman rose stiffly, standing tall in the sickly light. 'I'm sorry you feel the way you do, Jordan, and I assume you would take it kindly if I just got out of your life again and let you be?'

'Exactly,' she answered.

'Hey, let's not get hasty here, folks,' Joe Delta intervened. 'Look, Bannerman, you are getting all hurt and high and mighty, while you, Jordy, you're just the same. You're prepared to just let him go when he knows nothing about what happened to you or how you came to wind up here like this, tied up with a no-account like yours truly and turning cheap tricks for whiskey money. Seems the least we can have here is a little up-front truth and frankness. Or am I reading you wrong, Mr Big? Would you just rather walk than know your sister's real story?'

'No . . . no by glory I would not,' Bannerman said slowly.

'Jordan?'

'No. It would not make any difference,' the woman replied. 'It's not a pretty story, and you would just be judgmental and critical and superior as you always were—'

'Try me,' Gene cut in, resuming his seat. 'I want to know, Jordan, need to. Maybe it will help me understand.'

'Very well, but just remember, you insisted.'

'Attagirl,' Delta exclaimed, plainly pleased of any diversion or distraction which might delay his return to Keylock. 'Better dig out one of those fancy stogies of yours, Bannerman. And light me one while you're at it. Come to think on it, this here is a story that should really fire up a big American hero like yourself. Go ahead, Jordy, give it to him with both barrels.'

And she did.

CHAPTER 2

SOUTH OF THE BORDER

They met in Laredo a decade earlier when Señor Diego Rivera of Portales Province, cattleman and politico, came north to Texas to conduct a protracted legal battle with a Laredo beef packing company. The court case, which was finally decided in the Mexican's favour with compensating heavy damages, occupied several months during which Rivera, even though married with a family back home, met and fell in love with an American party girl, the most entrancing woman he had ever met.

Jordan Bannerman, who had changed her name to Terasina Jordan, was twenty-five years of age at the time, the darling of Laredo and courted by more eligible and mostly rich young Americans than she could rightly recollect.

But the handsome and dynamic Rivera swept her off her feet, they became lovers almost instantly and remained passionately involved until the wind-up of the big case, after which Rivera returned home to the bosom of his family, leaving Jordan heartbroken and in no doubt that it was all over.

She bore Rivera's child seven months later at the beginning of a black year for the father who lost two of his four sons in a stage accident in Mexico.

Although formally informed of the birth of Matthew James by letter from the mother, Rivera made no response to the news. Jordan did not hear from or see her child's natural father until two years later when, as newly installed governor of Portales Province, he tracked her down to a small cowtown on the Pecos where she was working as a schoolteacher.

Jordan was a survivor, a loving mother and a still beautiful woman. She was amazed when Rivera attempted to rekindle their affair, rejecting him out of hand. And only then, when forced to reveal his hand, was she stunned into disbelief to learn the real reason of his pursuit of her – and of Matthew James Jordan, aged two years.

With the loss of two of his sons and the surviving two boys now approaching manhood and showing alarming signs of bad character, the now Governor Rivera wanted their son, the child, to return to Mexico with him to be reared strictly and correctly in order that the governor might one day have a worthy successor to carry on his name and inherit his wealth.

Jordan could not believe it. But knowing Rivera's ruthlessness and power, she knew better than to not take him seriously. So she fled. Six weeks later in a little river town on the Rio, nightriders crossed the river from Mexico and removed her son by force. She had not seen Matthew James Jordan from that day to this.

When legal negotiations failed, the desperate mother scraped together what money she could manage and hired American mercenaries to travel to Portales Province and attempt to rescue her son.

The expedition proved disastrous with only two of the original six gunmen returning to Texas alive. By this, Jordan was broke, heartbroken and destroyed, and the bottle and the Crib Streets of the south became the blurred substitute life for the real one she had had taken from her.

End of story.

The sheriff of Hondo City was a lazy but obliging man of forty who was happy to take charge of Mr Bannerman's prisoner and proved quite ready to oblige in opening his files to dig out what he had available on the Matthew James Jordan abduction case.

The sheriff knew a great deal about the visitor from Keylock County, virtually all of it impressive. He felt happy in being able to help provide sufficient material on file to prove beyond any doubt that the grim story related by Bannerman's sister, and supported by Joe Delta was, in all important aspects, accurate.

'A bad business that abduction, Mr Bannerman,' the gaunt-ribbed badgepacker commented, leaning back in his chair as Gene continued to pore over the files. 'But of course incidents like this aren't all that uncommon along the borderlands. Americans go down there and stir up all kinds of devilment, they retaliate when and if they think they can get away with it. Plainly this Rivera was guilty of kidnap, and I sure feel for the mother, wherever she might be. But the fact of the matter is this man is big, with plenty of powerful friends in high places. For the US law to go in hard against him could trigger off trouble between Washington and Mexico City, and I can assure you that neither government would consider that just one kid could be worth all that uproar. In any case, Rivera is the father, no doubt about that, and I heard once his mother's just a lush. Could be the kid's a mile better off with daddy than mommy. Coffee, sir? You're looking peaked if you don't mind my saying so.'

Bannerman quit the law office soon after to walk the streets. It was now past midnight with a crescent moon hanging in the dark sky over Mexico. The Crib Street gun battle had roused the town, but now all was quiet and hushed with just the distant whistle of a locomotive coming in on the wind from the east.

Emotion had him in its grip as his way took him down by the river bridge, where old bums jungled up around little brushwood fires and the coyotes prowled close scavenging for scraps.

He knew Jordan had largely faded from his thinking over the years, and to encounter her again in such circumstances with such a story to tell had hit him hard.

She had a son. A Bannerman, even if he carried another name. His nephew, only grandson of Marsha and Matthew James Bannerman of Vickery County, Brazos River, victim of a ruthless Mexican *patrón* whose only claim to the child was having sired him. Deep down, he knew he was fighting a battle peculiar to somebody like himself. For he was a man of causes and missions who had unintentionally made a name for himself through helping the poor, fighting for the rights of what he called the Little People. His Camelot side – as his sister had liked to call it.

His sister had accused him of being more drawn to the excitement, adventure and the escape they gave from day-to-day responsibilities than by philanthropy. It never bothered him. He did what he did.

He knew what he wanted to do right now: head for Portales Province and bring back his sister's child. But for what reason? Simple kindness? To try and compensate for the pain Jordan had been through and because she had never felt she could turn to him? If in this he was being motivated by his 'Camelot side', what of it? It was nothing new.

The way he figured, why should folks go to the sheriffs, judges, the army or the government if they treated you like dirt? The least he might give a person was good advice, more often than not it was considerably more. He didn't see himself as any kind of do-gooder or philanthropist, just a somebody who cared.

He knew many suspected his reasons, believing there had to be ulterior motives in his generosity, always cynically searching for the hidden motivation for his concern for the rights of good people. He had been accused of glory-hunting when he created his organization, named the Family of Friends, whose activities at times overlapped or even replaced formal authority.

His response was always the same. Was it a crime to help people who could not help themselves? Why, if you happened to be rich and successful, were you expected to go for ostentatious luxury and high-living when there were fine Americans out there in desperate need of a helping hand?

People like his sister.

He stood on a street corner, still not sure. Then he reminded himself belatedly just how long it had been since he'd slept, how long he'd been fighting off exhaustion. Eight hours solid sleep would surely set him up and enable him to make the right decision, he decided, and headed off to the Railroad Hotel where he proceeded to sleep through until halfway down the next afternoon.

Delta stopped rapping out a snappy finger beat on his tobacco tin when the sheriff returned. He wasn't sure he liked the expression on the badgeman's homey mug. One way or another, he'd had a great deal to do with lawmen over the years and it had gotten so that more often than not he could read them like a book.

He jumped up from his cot and stretched, a long lean man with the suggestion of coiled whipcord in his body, a face that was at once comely and cunning, reflecting a keen yet dangerous intelligence.

'What's the good news, Sheriff? Wife run off but left behind all your dinero?'

The sheriff sauntered across to the cell and leaned a shoulder against the bars. He surveyed the pink telegraph slip between his fingers with a smile.

'Confirmation on you from the Keylock law, hardcase. Attempted rape and attempted murder, just as Mr Bannerman stated.' He looked up, the smile fading from washed-out hazel eyes. 'You really are a prime grade son of a bitch, aren't you, Delta?'

'Hey, don't believe all you hear, man. She was enjoying it until her old man showed up unexpected. Then she started to holler, he turned ugly, I had to dust him off.'

'You nigh killed him.'

'Nigh is right. The geezer's still breathing. Know why, teniente? I shot him to stop him coming at me with a hammer. But I aimed to wound. I could've killed him – easy as that.' He snapped his fingers. 'I am the best six gun shot you ever did see. I never miss what I aim for. That broken down assay agent's alive today because of Joe Delta, yet you and Mr Big just want to see me swing. Is that fair – I ask you?'

The sheriff made to turn away, but hesitated. 'I've heard about Bannerman doing things like this. Taking on folks' troubles and sticking his neck out. He's a curious one that. Impressive as hell, but curious.'

'He's a grandstanding, interfering, dung-eating lizard. And with luck, before he gets me back to Keylock, I'll get the jump on him and cut off his head and sell it to a man I know who runs a carnival.'

With a snort of disgust, the sheriff returned to his desk. But the prisoner was repentant.

'Sheriff, Sheriff, can't you tell when a man is sounding off just for the fun of it? I'm all talk. I've never killed a man who didn't have it coming. And Bannerman is straight even if he is a big-head and a show pony. I wouldn't harm the man even if he might walk me up a gibbet. Hell! He's my woman's brother. What would it do to my love life if I should blow him ass over backwards? And how's that pot going on your stove there anyway?'

The lawman filled two pannikins and carried them back to the cell. Despite his revulsion he was intrigued by Delta and Bannerman and their connections with a Crib Street jade who had once made front-page news in south Texas in a strange case involving the present governor of Portales Province.

Making himself comfortable on a stool, he was content to fill in his time waiting for Bannerman to show trying to find out what made this wild one tick. He was waiting for Bannerman to come take Joe Delta off his hands, for despite his charm and wit and easy ways, the sheriff had him figured as about the most dangerous lawbreaker he'd ever had in his cells. The sheriff was an indifferent peace officer but was a first-class judge of men, and badmen.

The late breakfast-cum-luncheon at the diner had hit the spot, now all he needed was a glass of smooth sourmash and he would be ready to make his decision regarding his sister, even though he already sensed what it might be.

Hondo City watched Gene Bannerman go by, a tall and wide-shouldered man with long arms, and a way of carrying himself that caused him to stand out from the crowd.

Although only a handful had ever laid eyes on the big man from the north he was well known through the newspapers and by word of mouth. Yet even what was known was insufficient to dispel their curiosity about a man who seemed given to doing and saying things that other men, especially the wealthy class to which this rancher and businessman belonged, did not.

Bannerman and his Family of Friends frequently brought suits against public figures suspected of crime and corruption. He'd slugged it out with the cattle-rustling gangs of the seventies, was known to be a man with a huge following in the Keylock region even though regarded with suspicion and open enmity by many a powerful organization or citizen because of his tough methods of dealing with matters which they saw as none of his business.

Now he'd come to Hondo City, shooting it out with, then arresting a badman before anyone knew he was in town. Was it any wonder that shoppers and porch-sitters and dignified matrons paused in what they were about to follow his progress in the direction of Rogan's Bar, the buzz of conversations not starting up again until the tall figure was well past.

The street consensus proved favourable in the main, with comments such as, 'Now that looks like the sort of man this town needs to deal with all these fallen women and railroad scum the Line brought in.' Or, 'Couldn't figure how a ranchin' feller would get to run down and out-gun a bad-ass like that Joe Delta feller, but lookin' at Bannerman you kind of understand.'

But there were always the dissenters in any given situation and cinder-dusted Hondo City was no exception. As chance would have it, a serious critic of any celebrity intruding on what he honestly regarded as his town, just happened to be drinking doubles with friends at the long bar when Bannerman walked by and called for a shot. Danny Coe was a young man with old eyes, with husky chest and shoulders and a temperament that was never enhanced by strong liquor.

And curly-haired Coe was one of the few men in town who'd actually ever had dealings with the visitor to Hondo City; a long-ago incident which had seen a drunken, younger Danny boy literally kicked off the streets of Keylock by the same tall man sipping on his sourmash – just for dunking a citizen in a horse trough in a discussion over livery fees. Danny could scarce believe his luck.

Bannerman alone and far from home, still strutting about like the stud rooster in the henhouse with everyone eyeing him off like he was really something – and wild Danny Coe surrounded by his best pards, likely *hombres* one and all.

'Who?' he suddenly boomed with full lung power, turning every head in the place in his direction. 'Who in the name of all that's holy kicked the shit-can over?'

The silence that fell like a club was deafening.

Until one of Danny's bunch just had to snigger at his good buddy's 'wit'.

The giggle was infectious and the others joined in, stealing glances at Bannerman to see how he was taking it, then looking peeved when he appeared not to realize Danny's greeting was meant for him.

Bannerman studied his glass. He remembered Coe well enough, and was hardly surprised by the roughcase's reaction. The thing was, he wasn't interested in any trouble, and had in fact been seriously considering going to visit with his sister just so soon as he'd finished his drink.

It galled him to allow this bum's taunt to go unanswered, but that was what he was planning to do as he drained his glass and reached for his hat which he'd placed upon the bar.

'Hey, you ain't leavin' are you, Bannerman? Glory be but you wasn't in no hurry to move on that day up north when you had a hundred boot-lickers behind you to back your grandstand play, were you – shit-kicker?'

Bannerman looked down, set his empty glass aside, turned.

Danny Coe looked bigger than he recalled, barrel-chested and slim-hipped in double-breasted flannel shirt and narrow-legged jeans pants. Bushy-haired and maverick-eyed, he now sported a thick dark moustache waxed at the tips beneath that crooked snout busted in a long-ago dust-up, maybe the one-sided one he'd featured in with a rancher on the streets of Keylock.

'Hello, Coe.' Gene's dark blue gaze was blank, his

30

tone neutral. He still wished to avoid trouble, yet at the same time was aware of the aggravation and contempt he intuitively felt towards this breed. Danny Coe did not belong to his favoured categories of little people or good people. His category was very plainly, horse's ass.

Coe glanced over his brawny shoulder to see his good pals ranging up in back of him. Four of them. He turned back to Bannerman and saw but one man. He fingered the handle of his low-slung six-shooter, inflated his chest and hooked his catfish mouth up at the corners.

'Hello? That the best you can do for an old sparrin' partner, Mr big-shot son of a whore, sir? Heck, I'm certain you can be a whole lot more polite than that.'

'Better get out of my way, Coe.'

'OK, sure, why not? A fair enough request. Tell you what, Bannerman, only thing that riles me about you today is them big shiny Colts you are wearin'. Notice how they catch the light? I gotta tell you, Mr Bannerman sir, that that glare is hurtin' my eyes somethin' fierce. Sure you wouldn't mind shuckin' them if a man asked perlite, would you?'

A percentage girl laughed shrilly.

Danny's pards were looking proud of their leader, mighty proud.

'Well, big man?' To show just how cool and in control he was, Danny stuck a crooked black cigar in his mouth and set it alight. In the glow of the vesta flame, his deeply bronzed skin was smooth and healthy. He shook the match out, blew smoke into

31

Bannerman's face. 'Can you help me with my problem?'

'Afraid not.'

Danny Coe nodded seriously, yet deep smile creases cut his smooth cheeks. Bannerman just stood easily before him with his feet set apart, long arms hanging loosely. Rogan's bar was tombstone quiet and Rogan was shaking like a rag weed in an August windstorm.

'So, where do we stand now?' Coe pondered aloud. 'If you won't oblige me by getting shook of them fancy cutters, could be someone could take them off of you, huh?'

'Could be.' Bannerman rested his hands back against the leading edge of the bar now. 'But who is to do it?'

Coe's eyes changed colour. He lunged forward, swinging from the floor. Bannerman's arms blurred and the distinct sound of crunching blows rocked the room as two iron fists smashed into the hard-case's face.

As he grabbed his nose and saw the blood, Coe's eyes went loco. He dropped into a crouch, muscular arms pumping as he parried for an opening, his forward shuffle cornering Bannerman against the bar. Gene's hands whipped behind him. He seized the bar edge, levered himself high, then lashed out with high-heeled boots to take Coe square in the chest with the brutal double kick.

The man rocketed back to crash into his startled bunch before thudding to the boards. Before any man could move, Bannerman was holding his right hand Colt and calmly replacing his hat.

'Don't even think about it, scum,' he advised. 'I went gently on Coe but couldn't promise the same thing for the rest of you.'

The hellers stared down at Coe who looked half-dead. They backed away as Bannerman came forward. 'When and if he comes to, tell him thanks, boys. I think I might have been about to make a decision that would have resulted in my going easy on a certain low-life scum down Mexico way. But meeting up with Danny boy was a reminder that a man can not rightly allow vermin like you to get away with anything. Not ever. Now get the hell out of my way while you can still walk.'

The four jumped back like well-drilled soldiers, which drew a titter of mocking laughter all around. But nobody spoke until Bannerman had left, and when someone looked out they saw he was making south for Crib Street.

CHAPTER 3

THE SAVAGE ONES

The boy rattled a stick along the bars of the cage but the jaguar failed to respond. It continued to pace the perimeters of its compound, padding with the heavy, slope-shouldered and effortless way cats have. Although the man coughed loudly and Matthew James raised a clanging stick-against-steel clatter again, they were ignored by the jaguar exhibiting his lofty feline arrogance; they did not exist for it on this late afternoon on San Cristobal Rancho.

'Do you know why he ignores us?' asked Diego Rivera.

'Because he does not like us?'

'He hates us, as you and I would hate anyone who put us in a cage.'

'Then if he hates us why isn't he angry with us?'

'Beneath his indifference he is angrier than you or I could be if we tried forever. Angry enough to tear us to pieces, then race to the hacienda and tear out the throat of everyone there, including Moma Luz.'

'Would he kill Maria?'

'Quick as a kiss.'

'Then I hate it . . . Maria is my friend.'

A frown briefly shadowed the powerful bearded face of Diego Rivera, and for a moment he was diverted from the small life lesson he was seeking to impart to the handsome child.

'Maria is but a servant, Matthew James. The high-born do not befriend servants or peasants.'

'But I like her.'

'Well, perhaps. But you love your mama and papa.'

'*Sí*, of course, Papa.'

'Of course.' The man returned his attention to the jaguar, just one of many beautiful animals housed in his large private zoo on the rancho. The heavily-muscled cat continued to circle her cage as though she were on an enormous journey across the sierras. 'So, why does she pretend not to notice us when she hates us and wishes to kill us?'

'I do not know.'

'Then you must understand. The jaguar is cunning and very cruel. It believes that by ignoring us we might be tempted do something foolish to attract her attention, such as moving closer than this railing to the bars where she might grab us and rip out our living hearts. This is deception, boy, and many people are as deceptive and dangerous as the jaguar. You must learn how to tell when they – cats or people – do not love you and may do you harm if you are careless or too trusting. Do you understand?'

'Perhaps.' The child's face was momentarily troubled. He loved the zoo and felt important whenever his busy father took time to be with him and give him lessons. Maria might teach him how to read and write but his father gave him lessons in what he called the school of life. But days like this when the late sun slanted down and the birds of prey screeched while the great cats prowled and growled about their enclosures, Matthew James Rivera, youngest and sixth child of Governor Rivera and his wife the Doña, and fourth surviving offspring, just wanted to play and enjoy the fun of having his father all to himself for a time.

He said, 'Can we see the monkeys now, Papa?'

'If you wish.' The man was mostly silent during the time spent at the monkey enclosure; he saw few parallels between the human and the simian and in truth did not wish to connect them in the child's thinking. Monkeys might be fun but Diego Rivera saw life as a serious matter in which the strong dominated the weak. The killer cats were strong and so was he; and so wished his youngest son to be.

The leopard was a disappointment to the boy, smaller than the jaguar and seemingly docile, even though his father insisted it was a great and successful killer of men.

Hoofbeats.

Man and boy turned from the leopard cage to see Rivera's sons and Matthew James's stepbrothers come riding up past the iguanas and the boas on their fine horses in their splendid clothes.

The boy moved a little closer to the father, whose smooth brow now creased in a taut frown. For Paulo

36

and Tomas Rivera, younger survivors of the rancho's blood feud with an adversarial ranchero which had claimed the lives of siblings Pedro and Dominic, were supposed to be at work on the western pastures with the foreman that afternoon, and their father prized duty and obedience above most anything.

As the lithe young men stepped down to tie up their horses by the tiger enclosure, a figure emerged from the lush growth higher up. It was an impressive American who was as familiar a sight around the ranch headquarters as Rivera himself.

Cody Mears was Rivera's personal bodyguard, and it never ceased to grieve the rich *ranchero* that he should need such protection right here in the heart of his empire.

The sons approached. Both were slender, arrogant and handsome, typical products of an indulged upbringing. And although they greeted their father with respect, there was a reserve in their manner as they stood before him, each waiting for the other to explain the reason why they were here.

Rivera fingered his moustache. 'Well?'

Paulo, the eldest, cleared his throat. 'We wish to visit Morelos, *patrón.*'

'And why is that?'

Tomas said, 'We have been working hard, the day has been hot and there is a dance.'

'Where would we be if we all were prepared to deny our duty for such petty reasons?' Rivera made a dismissive gesture. 'No. Return to the pasture. If you are late for the evening meal I shall know you are working late to compensate for the time you have lost making this foolish errand. Go.'

Tomas turned away with a sigh but Paulo's narrow face flushed darkly. 'I regret your response does not satisfy me, *patrón*,' he snapped. 'We are grown men, not children. I demand that—'

'Demand?' Rivera cut in, bristling. 'My children do not demand of me. Nobody does. Go now before I lose my temper.'

'And do what?' Paulo challenged hotly. 'Whip us as you did when we were small? As you never do him?' He was glaring balefully at Matthew James who clung to his father's trouser leg.

The scene was on the verge of turning ugly when Tomas tugged his brother by the sleeve and said, 'No more, Paulo, we must not go too far.'

But Paulo Rivera seemed ready to take it farther until the crunch of boots on gravel behind diverted his attention.

'Everythin' OK, Governor?'

The Americano gunman Cody Mears spoke softly but his face was hard as he met the brothers' eyes. Paulo glared at him for a long moment, but another touch from his brother seemed to draw the anger out of him, like stroking a savage dog.

Their backs rigid with anger, the brothers strode back up the slight rise to their horses to fling astride and spur away, the dust of their going drifting across the tiger enclosure, hazing in the low sunlight.

'*Gracias*, Cody,' Rivera murmured, and the body-guard walked away, his walk reminding the child of that of the leopard they had just been watching.

Matthew James looked a question at his father. He

did not understand much of what happened between the grown-ups but always sensed the tension in the air whenever his father and his stepbrothers were together.

He relaxed when Rivera smiled and took his hand. '*Por nada*,' he said. 'It is nothing. Come, we have one last visit to make.'

They bypassed the hawks and buzzards to finally halt before the largest enclosure of them all and Matthew James's favourite, the home of the Bengal tigers.

Mama Rivera still sometimes bitterly complained of the massive expense of keeping animals such as these, but at such times her husband just laughed tolerantly and insisted they were worth ten times the price he'd had to pay. The boy agreed.

Coal black and hot orange against the sunlight and shadow of the cage, the tigers were to him huge and improbably beautiful creatures whose ability to seemingly disappear into their background encouraged the notion in his mind that they were not like the other flesh-and-blood animals and birds but were rather mystical and magical, fabulous creatures of the imagination.

Today the tigers were drowsy and lazy, moving about sluggishly on huge padded feet, occasionally showing their teeth in soundless growls, neither ignoring nor taking particular notice of their visitors. Just like royalty, as his father sometimes said.

'What are the tigers thinking, Papa?'

'Nobody ever knows what a tiger thinks, boy.'

'Are they the greatest of all?' asked Matthew

James, knowing the answer.

'The very greatest.' A pause. Then, 'And you and I – Matthew James, and Diego Rivera – we are tigers.'

The boy believed him. And why shouldn't he? For everyone said his father was the greatest man in all Mexico. And the wisest.

'Hey, handsome, come on in and have some fun.'

With the slow dying of the day Crib Street was beginning to come to life, the girls appearing in their lamplit doorways to call softly to the men passing by, the rhythm of the pimps' gaudy house without walls sounding as it did every night for every farm girl from Tyler, every peroxide blonde from San Antonio and every single coaltown or cotton-mill cutie who had run away from home to make her mark on the world, only to wind up on one Crib Street or another – like a taunting droning blues song to which they knew every single word: you've been up, now you're down. You've been bought and paid for. Rented by the minute, sometimes by the hour. Nothing will every get better; things can only get worse. Now everything goes no matter how bad, just so long as it keeps away the Crib Street blues. It was whiskey, it was cocaine; it was the long opium dream. It was fighting in the alleyways and falling on the floor – everything to give now and not a thing to lose. Who wouldn't get the blues?

Girls from the big towns found the life of the cribs rougher and harder than the girls from the land. Farm girls and ranch girls took life mostly as it came and didn't expect too much of it. But the mining town and plantation workers from the east took to it easiest of all. Hard times and rough treatment meant nothing to them – this was the only life they knew.

Every time a company padlocked a mine gate, or cotton prices plummeted in Louisiana, a fresh flock of girls jumped the railroads west to start working on the Crib Streets for the price of a meal and a bottle of gin. Sometimes it was only for the gin, as it was for Terasina Jordan, who wasn't calling softly to any passer-by tonight, wasn't even showing herself in the doorway for fear that some cowboy, railroader or visiting salesman might like the look of her and stop by to lay his money down.

Tonight she sat at the table in the dim light drifting in from the street with a bottle in one hand and a framed photograph of a baby in the other, too drunk to work and too bitter to cry.

Her mind worked sluggishly as she attempted to sort out everything that had happened here in the past from what had taken place just in the last twenty-four hours.

Until finally she had it straight: Joe and her brother. That was what had sent her reaching for the bottle again tonight. The Matthew James pain was always there but Joe and Gene, that was something new and raw.

She took a pull on the bottle and leaned back in the hard chair. She knew full well that Joe Delta was no good; nobody had to tell her that. Who else but a no-good would be interested in a woman like her? And he was interested and kept on proving it in his erratic careless way.

Yet she was deeply out of sorts with her behind-bars boyfriend tonight, for it was Delta's landing in hot water up north that had put her brother on his tail, and in desperation he had come running to her looking to hide with her on Crib Street.

Now Gene knew it all.

Not that she gave one good damn, she told herself. Why should she care what Mr High-and-mighty Sir Lancelot might think about her? Even as children she had been puzzled and alienated by his attitude towards life. Like he was on a mission to make good, save the West and God alone knew what else, while all she had ever wanted was a man to love and a child of her own to hold in the silver morning light.

They were chalk and cheese and she thought it typical that his reappearance in her life should coincide with his taking Joe out of her life, maybe to serve a long stretch in jail, maybe to hang. He was still do-gooding and interfering and making her feel inferior and inadequate as he had done throughout their Brazos River childhood and beyond.

She was raising the bottle to her lips when she sensed a presence. She'd heard nothing but knew someone was there. Her instincts seemed so unnaturally heightened by grief and gin and self pity that, even before she turned her head, she knew who it was.

The tall figure filled her doorway in silhouette, and she lifted her bottle in mocking salute.

'Beat the shields and light the braziers,' she slurred. 'For the knight errant returneth to rescue the fair damsel.' Her tone turned harsh. 'Only she doesn't want to be rescued, especially not by . . . by. . . .' She had lost her train of thought. The bottle that was half empty had been full when she began.

She appeared dazed and uncertain as Bannerman came in removing his hat. There was enough street light to see by but not enough for him to see how ravaged and drunken she looked. Seated there at her solitary table, she could have been his kid sister of years ago, everybody's darling.

'Might I sit down, sis?'

'Sit, go . . . who cares?'

He placed his hat upon the table and filled the second chair. He sat in profile to her watching the doorway. He always faced the door. Gene Bannerman made his money raising beef cattle and bankrolling big deals in lumber, copper and cotton. But because of his preoccupation with the have-nots and the troubles they fell into, he had fashioned an alternative reputation in dangerous circles, as typified by his violent clash in Rogan's Bar. He had come down on too many hardcases and terminated too many violent lives to ever take the chance that some gunkid with a grudge might not come blazing through an unwatched doorway.

'I've been thinking, Jordan.'

'Strange, so have I.'

'About what happened to you and . . . and the boy.' He glanced at the photograph on the table, then raised his eyes to her dim face. 'You should have come to me.'

'I didn't know where you were in those days.'

'You could have found me had you really tried.'

'Finding fault with baby sister again, brother dear?'

'I would have helped you.'

'How was I supposed to know that? When I saw you last, you were mostly only talking about going to war for your damned little people against a big cruel world. You were mostly talk. By the time I realized brother Gene had gotten to be both rich and famous for fighting other people's battles, it was too late.' She looked away. 'I think it was always too late for little Matthew James. A body might as well try and fight the government as Rivera. . . .'

'He's just a man.'

'Just a man with a governorship and a million dollars.' Jordan tossed her head. 'It's pointless talking about it, Gene. My son is gone and I'm finished. You can't do anything for either of us now.'

Bannerman fell silent for a long thoughtful time, emotions warring beneath his tailored grey vest with heavy gold watch chain. What was gestating in his mind, the half-formed resolution which had overtaken him at Rogan's, was far different from anything he had attempted before. In his time he'd gone after rustlers and road agents, crooked operators, conmen, the occasional killer, even a corrupt army officer diddling the system. There were scars to show for these digressions from his everyday life at spread and office, and doubtless he would earn more of the same in the future, or for as long as he believed he could make a difference.

But from the moment he'd learned about Jordan's child and Diego Rivera he had been aware that this was something vastly different.

For the man was, as she had just pointed out to him, provincial governor of Portales – the region's largest *ranchero* complete with a well deserved reputation as a strong man. Nobody messed with Diego Rivera with impunity; Bannerman was familiar enough with life in northern Mexico to know that.

For any man to set out with the intention of taking Rivera on on his home turf, and seeking to take from him something he obviously prized so highly, might to many seem the height of absurdity.

But then the younger man in him posed the question: had King Arthur flinched from the odds when faced with a duel to the death with the giant of St Morgan's Mount? He shook his head irritably. He was no longer the youthful idealist who could be influenced by such allusions, he chided himself. Perhaps all the Arthurian history was just myth and legend, but what he was contemplating now was immediate and hard-edged reality. In plain terms, he had to decide if Gene Bannerman was prepared to die attempting to help a sister who despised him, for a child he didn't even know.

But then understanding came over him like a wave and he saw it all with sudden clarity. That he had been meant to track Joe Delta to Jordan's door, that fate had decreed he should come into her shattered life right now and had handed him a once in a lifetime opportunity to save his only kinfolk.

This was not going to be some swashbuckling adventure played out for God alone knew what obscure ideal. He was looking at a chance to both do something worthwhile and perhaps in the process revive a family more vital and close than the Family of Friends he had surrounded himself with at Keylock.

Real kin. Flesh and blood. Surely there had never been a 'knight of the realm' who would turn his back on such a quest. He rose, looming tall against the low rafters.

'I'm going to bring your boy back, sis.'

He was astonished when she burst into tears. He'd thought her too far gone for tears. He wanted to reach out and touch her shoulder but feared her rejection.

'I can do it,' he said to reassure her.

'If you do anything it will be to get my son killed. You don't know Diego—'

'No harm will come to the boy. You have my word.'

She stared up at him with tears streaming down her face.

'I was right before, wasn't I? You are still playing God. Well, you are not playing with my child's life, I won't allow it.'

But he was already moving for the door. A decision had been made, a line drawn. There had never been a greater opportunity to uphold the things he believed in, and now it was irresistible. He could feel the south tugging at him. Smelt the dust and adobe and the dry winds of Mexico. The ultimate challenge!

'So long, Jordan.'

The flung gin bottle smashed against the doorframe splashing him with liquor.

'Go, stay, die, disappear! Who cares, Gene, who

cares? You certainly never did. About anybody. All you ever cared about was how fine you are and how grand people think you are. You are worse than ever now and I curse the day Joe dragged you back into my. . . .'

The drunken voice faded. Bannerman was walking away, long arms swinging, staring straight ahead. None of the half-naked girls leaning in their doorways called to this one. To their knowing glances it was plain he was no client. What he looked like was a man bent on destruction, but whether it was of himself or some other it was impossible to guess in the misting, drifting Crib Street night.

CHAPTER 4

JAILHOUSE BLUES

The long jail hours were weighing heavy on Joe Delta's shoulders as he sat on the edge of his cot flicking playing cards into his upturned hat on the floor.

'Twenty-three,' he counted as the five of diamonds sailed into the crown. Flick. 'Twenty-four.' Flick. 'Bastard! Can't get to twenty-five. Hey, lawdog! You still sleeping, you loafer? The town's afire and I'm making love to your wife.'

No response from the slumped figure in the chair with the newspaper covering his face.

Running the jailhouse in Hondo City was a relaxed affair for the incumbent sheriff. The day the first train pulled in to disgorge half a hundred hustlers, grifters, twisters, phonies, painted women and white-fingered gambling dudes with sneak guns in their shorts, this badgeman had realized he was hopelessly outnumbered and responded accordingly.

He gave up.

Now, when gunfire erupted or some citizen might come staggering in with a bloody nose and a story of crime and violence, the sheriff was nowhere to be found. When things were quiet, as they had been tonight ever since the set-to at Rogan's, he might take a constitutional along the walks or maybe catch forty winks at the office. He was a boring and gormless man, and the fact that Delta wanted him to wake up just to relieve the boredom told the prisoner just how desperately bored he really was.

He almost wished Bannerman would get himself together and escort him back to Keylock. At least he wouldn't be bored when they charged him with rape and attempted murder and tried to fit a yellow rope about his neck.

He sighed as he rose and went to his window. Against the fall of night the barn next door thrust its stone and log shoulder, its dark mass blotting out the stars. Halfway up the wall loomed a heavy oak beam which served as a hoist for bales of hay stored in the loft. He'd been told a lynch mob had busted a prisoner out of this drowsy badgeman's *calabozo* last winter and the oak beam barn hoist had served as an impromptu gallows.

There had been rumours here that they might lynch him because he was an alleged rapist, but thus far nothing had come of it.

The prisoner was none too scared. For one, he doubted this dirty town had the guts to try anything on a Bannerman prisoner. For another, he'd never figured to make it to any ripe old age anyway so why the heck should he care?

But melancholy settled over him as he lighted one up and dragged deep, gusting smoke clouds towards the hanging brass lamp. When he went, he'd hoped to go down in a blaze of glory, not gurgling and choking with his tongue hanging out two feet while a couple of hundred crackerheads jeered and laughed.

Even after his little bit of boisterous fun up in Keylock he'd never imagined his days might be numbered – until that tall geezer in grey got after him.

He sighed gustily. Had he suspected what he was in for he might have ambushed Bannerman and blown his uppity head clear off his shoulders. Had he suspected. . . . But he hadn't, and that damned dogooder had nabbed him. He'd still dearly love to give him six up close, but did not fancy his chances.

He shook his head wonderingly thinking about the influence Bannerman exercised in these parts. The town of Keylock hadn't bothered chasing Joe Delta, but a big rancher had. There was no talk of Keylock law coming for the prisoner. Bannerman would handle that too, no doubt. Yet if he was such a freaking wonder at interfering with the rights of wild ones like himself, he marvelled, why wasn't the big rich bastard wearing a badge? The bitterness gripped him savagely. Caught, jugged and bottled by a citizen, not a lawman! Who would have ever expected such a fate for fast Joe Delta?

A shoulder hit the jailhouse door and the man

he'd been thinking on came striding in like he owned the place.

'Change of plans, Sheriff,' he announced as the lawman blinked awake. 'I'm unable to escort Delta back to Keylock so I'll leave it to you to arrange his transportation with them up there.'

He swung across to the cells and Delta blew smoke in his face.

'I'll supply them with a deposition on your apprehension and all I know about you, mister,' he stated with an air of finality. 'I won't say it's been a pleasure as it hasn't been. But I can rest assured you won't be fouling up my sister's life for a good twenty years, if ever.'

'Bannerman, Bannerman – you're all twisted and wrong-headed. I'm the best thing Jordan has going for her. I'm the only geezer who gives a cuss about her, and that includes her big crazy brother. And at least she turned to me way back when she had the big trouble with the greaser, not you. Doesn't that tell you something, Mr Big?'

Gene's eyes narrowed. 'Somehow I can't imagine you doing anything for anybody, mister. Jordan didn't say—'

'What I did for her? Why should she? She doesn't owe you anything. But just for the record, big man, I shelled out some hard money and put my neck on the line for your sister that time while you were—'

'She told me about sending men south after her boy,' Bannerman frowned. 'Are you saying you were involved?'

The prisoner chuckled. 'Involved? It was my show,

Mr Top-Lofty. I recruited the men, I took them to the province. . . .' His words trailed off and his shoulders slumped. 'I planted the bodies and led the way home with my tail between my legs when Rivera slit us up a real treat.'

It was a long slow time before Bannerman responded.

'I . . . I didn't know. . . . What can you tell me about Rivera and his set-up down south, mister?'

'Why for?'

'It should be obvious. I'm going down there, of course.'

Delta's ears pricked and he was suddenly serious. 'After the kid?'

'Of course.'

'You're meat.'

'What?'

'Rivera will gut you and string your innards from Christmas to breakfast.'

'Better men have tried. Now come on, speak up, man, I don't have all night.'

'You're really serious, ain't you? Well, if that's the case, let's do a deal, man. You want to help Jordan, so do I. You're talking of riding off into strange territory to get killed – I have been there and know Rivera's situation. You can set me loose and for that I'll do whatever I can to see you and the kid come back alive. You'll never get a better offer than that.'

'You are dreaming, hardcase.'

'You need me, Mr Big. Both for the reasons I just gave and another mighty important one.' He thrust a hand though the bars. 'Give me an iron.'

'Are you crazy?'

'Unloaded, man, unloaded. Come on, don't waste time. I'm about to clinch this deal I'm offering you.' He snapped his fingers. 'Gimme.'

Bannerman hesitated a moment longer. Then drew out a Colt and broke it open to dump the shells into his palm, the sheriff looking on with pop eyes. He passed the piece between the bars and the prisoner slid it into his empty holster. He stepped back and slipped into a crouch.

'Ready?' Bannerman nodded.

Delta's right hand whipped up from his side, caught the butt of the revolver and brushed it upward for his hand to close round it. At the same time his finger slipped into the trigger guard and his right thumb drew back the hammer, cocking it.

The piece whipped from leather and the muzzle was aimed at the centre of Bannerman's chest, the entire exercise executed with such blinding speed that only an educated eye such as Gene's could appreciate the skill involved.

'Pow!' Delta said, dropping the hammer on an empty chamber. He fanned the hammer and 'pow-powed' a further five make-believe shots before lowering the weapon with a big grin.

'I can shoot the eye out of a flying crow while you are wondering what day it is, Mr Big. So what do you say? Take out the biggest life insurance bargain anyone ever heard of by taking me along to at least give you half a chance against the governor and all his peons, *vaqueros*, *pistoleros* and family clan, or go off on your stiff-necked own and end up as fertilizer for

53

Rivera's prime cow pastures?'

Watching and listening in awed silence in the background, the sheriff didn't expect for a moment that Bannerman would give the offer a moment's consideration, but he was wrong about that. For Gene Bannerman sensed this could prove the most dangerous quest he'd ever taken on, believed it so strongly that he found himself ready to risk linking up with a dangerous man he detested for no better reason that he was faster with a six gun than anybody he'd ever seen.

Late the following night two dark riders swam their horses across the Rio Grande north-west of Laredo.

Joe Delta was first into Mexico.

'Maria, Maria!' called the boy, running down the broad breezeway, arms extended, dark curls tumbling. 'It is time for chocolate.'

The girl appeared in a doorway several doors along, sleeves rolled up and a scarf around her hair. There was always more work at the great hacienda than all the servants could rightly get through in a day, and Maria was a working girl. Yet if anything could tempt her away from duty it was the boy. They were crazy about one another, and if this puzzled the *patrón* and irritated the doña, then that was just the way it was. Twice Doña Luz had attempted to have the girl dismissed, but Matthew James kicked up such a fuss that Rivera had decided it simply wasn't worth the trouble. 'Besides,' he had persuaded his wife, 'she is the best housemaid we ever had, and can be trusted.'

It was the trustworthy aspect which finally won the doña over, for mistrust and the uncertainty associated with it may well have been the darkest cloud hanging over this great house.

The girl swung the boy into her arms and he laughed with delight. It was one of those quieter days when the men were out on the range in the dust and heat leaving house servants, cooks and yard hands free to get on with their domestic chores relatively undisturbed.

Setting Matthew James down, Maria removed her scarf and a mass of dark hair fell free to her shoulders. 'Hot milk or cold, *bello?*'

'Cold . . . race you.'

They sped down the breezeway together, the girl long-legged and graceful, the child putting everything he had into it. They ran past the huge rooms, dimmed by oleanders and drawn yellow blinds, furnished with massive mahogany and cedar chairs and tables resting upon gorgeously coloured rugs, skipped past the fat old washing woman with the cigar in her mouth, darted on by the suit of armour worn by a conquistador, the library, the laundry, the parlour and then the kitchen door – which the boy reached just inches ahead.

The head cook was a stern and sober eminence so the pair calmed down and entered the vast room properly, as a shadow fell across the glass door by the end of the breezeway. Cody Mears appeared against the sunlight flooding down into the garden, bareheaded and neatly dressed with the customary two Colts thonged to lean thighs.

Moving silently to the kitchen doorway, he glanced in to see Maria and Matthew James busy at the work bench with milk and chocolate. The American's flat grey eyes met those of the cooking staff, then he moved on along the breezeway, a fairheaded and wide-shouldered presence in this house filled with people all darker than he save for the light-skinned boy.

The gunman was the most highly paid employee on San Cristobal and certainly the most dangerous. Although his official designation was that of Rivera's personal bodyguard, times like this when the *ranchero* was engaged elsewhere and Matthew James was in the house, Cody Mears invariably stayed close to the child.

His unofficial designation, as his employer so often reminded him, was that of Matthew James's guardian. Although Rivera had never said so in as many words, it was understood by the American that the father believed his son could be at some risk at the hands of unspecified persons within the ranch itself, as well as those outsiders who might wish him harm for one reason or another.

But if this aspect of his employment was not completely clear, Mears' duties certainly were. Should any person on San Cristobal attempt to harm the child in any way, regardless of whom they might be, Mears was to shoot them dead on the spot.

All the ranch knew this, just as they knew Cody Mears was a gentlemanly, quietly spoken and cold-blooded killer. And so it was assumed by most if not all that the little boy was safe here in his father's kingdom of grass, cattle and farmlands sprawled at the foot of the sierras, while Mears himself saw the price of this security as his eternal vigilance.

The gunman was in the third of the four walled courtyards when Maria and Matthew James appeared, the boy toting a mug of chocolate-flavoured milk.

Every male on the ranch was aware of Doña Luz's handsome housemaid who, despite her Indian blood or perhaps because of it, was freely regarded as the most striking looking female within a hundred miles. The Yaqui strain showed in Maria's long legs and bluish-black hair and in the full, bold curve of the mouth. Slanted green eyes were lighter than her olive complexion, to which they provided sharp contrast. The rest of her, at nineteen years of age, was only what might be expected by Spanish-Indian good looks well seasoned by the Mexican sun.

'*Buenos días*, Maria,' the gunman called across the hot morning.

The response was a faint nod. It was said on the ranch that in her own way, Maria was just as aloof and proud as the Riveras themselves. This caused her to be viewed both as a mystery and source of annoyance to the bucks and would-be suitors who got absolutely nowhere with her, not even arrogant and stylish *hombres* like Cody Mears.

'Is the boy well?' he called.

'He is always well when he is with me, *señor*.'

Mears understood what was meant. Matthew James was distant with his stepmother and stepbrothers but warm and demonstrative towards his father. But a blind man could tell he loved Maria, and Mears believed this was easily explained. The kid had been taken from a young mother, and Maria was young and loving – only certainly not towards him. Hell, the kid liked him a lot more than she did.

'Hey, Matty,' he said. 'How's the boy?'

'Fine, Cody. Want some chocolate?'

'Another time, pardner.'

Mears would like to dally but instead moved off on his rounds. He was proud of his position as guardian to the province's first family, which was a far cry from shooting people for money on the dusty streets of Lubbock, El Paso or Santa Fe. And he wondered if when the governor returned from Morelos tonight, he might not suggest an increase because he was doing such a damned fine job. If Rivera doubted this, he reasoned, all he had to do was look at how safely he kept both him and his son. His favoured son.

By mid-afternoon when he quit the governor's palace on the plaza in Morelos, Rivera had had more than enough of signing papers, conferences, receiving petitions and decision-making. In truth the governorship did not go very deep with him; it was merely something he had acquired in order to boost himself even higher than ever in the eyes of the province. Mostly he left the day-to-day administrative chores to underlings, which left him free to pursue his real interests such as acquiring greater wealth and power, breeding blood horses, gambling and women.

A woman occupied the governor in a white house off the square for an hour. Then it was back into his gleaming carriage and four with mounted escort for the run down the valley to San Cristobal.

Leaning back against the velvet cushions as rubber-tyred wheels carried him smoothly and safely homewards, Diego Rivera, the man who had everything, frowned over an expensive cigar.

More rumours. Rumours that his bitter enemy from the valley beyond, the Texan born *ranchero* and malcontent Zeke Cromwell, was allegedly up to his old tricks of soliciting support amongst Rivera's rivals and inferiors to try and force him from office and then implement official investigations into his land titles and other 'questionable' aspects of the governor's private and public life.

Disturbing, if hardly surprising, considering the two's long enmity.

But just that day an informant had come forward with the information – cheap gossip Rivera was more inclined to label it – that both his sons, Paulo and Tomas, had recently been seen visiting Cromwell's Texas ranch.

He might not believe this but the governor knew he did not completely trust his sons, and had not done so in many years. They were a bitter disappointment. He saw them as sly, devious and overly ambitious, certainly not men to compare with the other two sons he'd lost in the last great battle with Cromwell.

They were the kind of progeny that could keep any father pacing the floor all night long about what might happen after he was gone. But Rivera had the counter to that concern, having foreseen the need for it years after learning he had a fifth son in Texas.

He leaned from the coach window and called to the driver, 'Faster, Guido, I promised my son we would ride to the river today.'

The coach picked up speed. On San Cristobal, whenever Rivera referred to his son in a certain loving way, all knew he did not mean either Paulo or Tomas.

CHAPTER 5

CAME THE TEXANS

'Looking at you, pardner.'

'Yeah.'

Joe Delta was relaxed but his tall companion was not as they stood leaning against the highly polished bar of the crowded Riata Cantina. The Americans had reached Morelos on Saturday night, and the town was bulging at the seams. A rodeo had been held during the day and the crowds had stayed in town to celebrate. Around the newcomers were pretty girls and swarthy horsemen, smiling Spanish drunks and skinny-hipped dancers twirling and stamping wherever they could find room. Gene Bannerman was uneasy; he wasn't sure why.

But as his eyes played over the crowd, cutting back here and there when he lighted on a certain face, a certain look, he began to understand.

He realized everything he saw beneath the coloured lamps of the Riata was not quite as boisterously free-wheeling as it had first appeared. There were men present without a grin to split up between them, Mexicans, a surprising number of expatriate Americans, one or two breeds in black shirts who didn't look as though they would contribute anything to any social occasion. Ever.

Yet realizing the atmosphere concealed an underlying tension paradoxically saw him begin to relax. For whatever was building here on this mariachi Saturday night, it plainly had nothing to do with them. And with a long day in the saddle behind him and plenty to occupy his mind now they were slap in the middle of Portales province, that was all that concerned him.

He sipped his brandy and it was good. Then he lighted a cigar, leaned an elbow on the bar and absorbed the sights and scents and sounds of Diego Rivera's world for the first time.

The Americans had sighted tangible evidence of Rivera's prominence *en route* to livery, hotel and finally the cantina. A large portrait of the governor mounted on an upper gallery of the walled palace was visible from the square, as it was intended to be. The Rivera name was to be seen above the doors of a bank, a hotel and several large merchant houses. And at the hitch rail outside, Delta had pointed out several blood horses bearing the scrolled SCR brand, Rivera's ranch.

Impressive stuff.

Yet Bannerman had expected nothing less. For years Rivera had been a significant figure, even in Texan eyes. A little cynically, he supposed only a man of this stature could have gotten away with a blatant kidnapping of a Texas citizen, due to the power he wielded and the strings he could pull.

'Hi, beautiful,' Delta greeted a sultry bar girl wearing a dress split thigh high.

' 'Allo, *señor*,' the girl replied in a husky voice but drifted right on by without giving any suggestion of recognition.

'Old friend of yours?' Gene asked sarcastically.

'Hell no, never saw her before.'

'Well, I guess it's a long time since you were here last.'

'Wouldn't make any difference if it was yesterday, pardner. Nobody here knows yours truly. Do you think I'd have ridden in here so big and brassy if they did?'

'But you said—'

'I said I brought a bunch of guns down here to raise hell and scare the crap out of Rivera, and that is just what I did.' The quick grin flashed. 'But I wasn't a foot soldier; I was the general. You savvy?'

'Better explain.'

Bannerman lowered himself to a stool as the brandy did its soothing work. Eyes black, blue, and in-between were watching him. He was the kind who attracted attention wherever he went with his height and bearing. Drinkers and pretty girls and hard-eyed old-timers were plainly trying to figure just who or what they might be, even though he was attempting to attract as little attention as possible. Looking from one *gringo* to the other, the same bystanders didn't seem to have much difficulty sizing up Joe Delta. He

63

looked typical of a breed all too familiar south of the border – hard, cocky and almost certainly trouble-some. They would rather contemplate the tall one in the fifty-dollar riding shirt.

'I knew right off that it would be tough down here,' Delta supplied, pivoting on his stool until his back was against the bar. 'Going up against Rivera, that was. I hired the best gunnies money and bullshit could come by and I plotted out a plan to grab the kid that a five star general would be proud of. But you see, pardner, I didn't want to cash in my chips down here. I was too young, too good looking. Hell, I was too me to croak at twenty-three on foreign dirt trying to pull off something impossible as a favour for a fine-looking woman.' He spread his quick hands. 'So, what did I do?'

'You're telling the story.'

'Simple. I did the brain work and organized the whole shebang, but when it came the night for the boys to split up, some to create a diversion out at the ranch while the others made it to the hacienda to grab the boy, I stayed where I'd been all along, out of sight. So they worked to my plan, did exactly what I ordered, fought the good fight and ended up shot to ribbons – exactly as they would've if I'd been with them.' He turned his curly head to look at Bannerman. 'Catch on now? Scarce anyone down here has ever seen me. Far as these rubes or Rivera is concerned, I'm a regular cleanskin like you. We are both checking in here with a clean slate.'

Bannerman was impressed. The more he saw of Delta the less he trusted him, yet the more of a real

64

operator he appeared to be.

'We will get the lie of the land and finger Rivera's weaknesses,' he said after draining his glass. 'And just so we have things straight, you did the planning last time you were down here, but I'll do it now.'

'You sure do pack some confidence, Mr Big, I will say that for you. But don't sweat. If you want to be the general, the job's yours. In the meantime . . . here she comes again.'

Sultry, slender and smoky-eyed glided up to them again and this time Delta was able to sweet talk her into accepting his offer to buy a round. Her name was Carla and although she smiled a lot at Delta's impudence she kept glancing at Bannerman, who barely noticed. He was listening to what she said in response to Delta's harmless questions, but his attention was elsewhere. Until she asked, 'Are you *gringos* here for the banquet?'

'And what banquet might that be, sexy?' Delta almost drooled. He was a different man with women about; his style and judgment seemed to go straight out the window.

'Out at the *gobernador's rancho* tomorrow,' she supplied. And looking straight at Bannerman, added coquettishly, 'You, Señor Gene, you look like one of those men who would be invited to break bread with Señor Rivera.'

He was considering this remark when the flat hard smack of a hand coming into contact with a face cut through the murmur of music and voices and chinking glassware, the first gust before the storm.

In a distant corner two groups of ranch riders, one

Mexican and the other American, had been arguing and throwing their arms about for some time. Bannerman and Delta didn't know they were opposing round-up gangs from the San Cristobal and Texas ranches, the cattle outfits of Diego Rivera and expatriate Zeke Cromwell respectively. Nobody seemed to know what the trouble might be, although Gene had already learned through Delta that the cattle barons had been at loggerheads years ago when he was here, and that nothing seemed to have changed.

A lean rider with a Texas twang was cussing out a bar girl who had handed him one right across the chops for some reason or another. Now a Rivera *vaquero* stepped in and gave the Texan a good shove back against the wall. Paradoxical, as any good woman can be at any time, the girl landed a high-heeled kick to the *vaquero*'s knee cap. The man howled, hopping round on one leg, then snatched up a glass and dashed the contents into the woman's face.

She screamed and the brawl erupted with an abruptness and volcanic fury which impressed even two visiting Americanos enjoying a quiet drink at the bar with Piedra the barkeep.

Soon Bannerman and Delta had reason to be thankful they had chosen the bar and not a table, as row after row of little tables and their occupants were engulfed by this tidal wave of spontaneous violence which continued to ebb and flow closer to the bar without ever quite reaching it.

Carla pretended to be frightened yet plainly had

cut her eye teeth on bar-room brawls. Even so, Delta slung a protective arm about her and laid wagers with some of the sports about him on the outcome, while the proprietor wrung his hands tragically and kept calling for someone to alert the law, although nobody seemed to hear.

It was obvious to Gene that the ruckus was losing momentum when two slender Mexicans in elegantly silver-trimmed riding gear and flat-brimmed black sombreros came through a side door to view the chaos with some alarm.

Delta leaned across to Bannerman to make himself heard. 'Rivera's sons. They haven't changed that much since I saw them last. You can pick them out by the hundred-dollar hats and the Arabs they ride to—'

His words were drowned out by the blast of Paulo Rivera's pistol as he drilled a shot into the rafters. As debris fell and the racket dropped by several decibels, his brother shouted: 'Cristobal riders, stop this immediately! Governor's orders!'

The saloon sighed with relief as the former combatants immediately began grinning and patting one another on the shoulder, like all they had been waiting for was one good reason to stop. But first Bannerman, then Delta, glimpsed the rat-faced American in the red shirt, lying on the floor with a blood-soaked head, dragging a six-shooter from his belt under the cover of a table and throwing down on the closest Rivera, snarling and foaming at the mouth.

'Stinkin' uppity greaser bastards!' he screamed,

and the head-jarring roar of the .45 rattled glassware and set women screaming as Tomas Rivera ducked under a howling slug.

The cowboy was up on one knee readying to trigger again as two fellow Americans went into action behind.

Bannerman and Delta were two men with but a single thought as they cleared their .45s. The Riveras were the governor's sons and they were suddenly in a position to come to their rescue – if they were quick enough.

They made certain they were. Just as each made certain he didn't kill anybody and maybe wind up on a Mexican gibbet.

Two Colts thundered in unison and the drunken cowboy shootist, his belligerence obliterated in a moment, dropped his smoking gun with a shriek of agony and rolled across the littered floor hugging a bleeding boot with one hand and a bullet-busted leg with the other.

Soon the man's whipped-dog whining sound was all that was to be heard in Riata Cantina as everyone in the place gaped across at the strangers from across the border like they were made of flypaper and their eyeballs were the flies.

With wisping tendrils of gunsmoke shrouding their faces, Joe and Gene traded looks in the deep well of silence. The thoughts of each man were identical.

Earlier, they'd spent a deal of time successively proposing and rejecting a dozen unsatisfactory plans for infiltrating San Cristobal quietly and as unobtrusively as possible. Plainly it shaped as a high-risk challenge no matter which way you looked at it. Both were experienced enough to appreciate the danger in any situation that required two Americanos showing up in Old Mexico with the express intention of kidnapping – that was the only word for it – the infant son of the most powerful and ruthless man in all the province.

In characteristic fashion, Delta had grown impatient at one stage and suggested that, as two fast guns with sand in their craw, they simply get out to the giant spread, infiltrate and blast their way to success, gunslinger-style.

To his credit, the badman had readily conceded that his 'plan' would almost certainly see them shot to dog meat for their trouble. So they'd settled for a quiet drink while they sussed out the lie of the land, evaluated the enemy's weaknesses and strengths before hopefully coming up with a strategy worthy of the name.

The sudden entry of Rivera's sons into the picture here which provoked the six gun reaction from the Cromwell rider who would answer to the name of Limpy for a long time to come, had sounded very much like opportunity knocking, and each had responded accordingly.

It was certain that if Limpy had not let fly at a Rivera, the two newcomers would have certainly kept their powder dry.

They were hardly surprised, yet certainly gratified, when after order had been fully restored and one bitter-cussing cowpoke packed off to the medicos, the Riveras dusted themselves off and crossed the room to offer their thanks.

Joe Delta was smart enough to say little and smile a lot during the meal that followed. It was obvious to the hardcase that the brothers, self-important and cold-eyed though they proved to be, even when in a grateful frame of mind, were responding to Bannerman's charm and eloquence much more readily than to his cynical, sardonic style.

During the *frijoles* and *chilli con carne* at the excellent eatery two doors along from the Riata, Delta heard more about art, Arthurian legends and some alien form of entertainment called opera than he really felt was good for him.

But Paulo and Tomas Rivera had been educated at a Jesuit college in the south and knew something about such things, and as members of the ruling class felt obliged to show their aristocratic credentials.

He studied the pair covertly as Paulo and Bannerman traded quotations from American and Spanish literature now. The Riveras were danger men, he decided, now he had the opportunity to view them up close. Lean, almost waspish with hungry-looking handsome faces, dark hair brushed high off the brow, alike enough to be identified as kin even by a stranger, the brothers radiated a common watchfulness of manner, and their movements were quick and graceful. They'd survived a close call less than an hour earlier, yet seemed to have quite recovered from the experience well before they checked out the dessert menu.

'The *teniente* will deal with that stinking *gringo*,'

insisted Tomas as he passed around the pre-strudel cigars. He made a cutting gesture in the air. '*Gringo* filth and excrement – er, no racial slight intended you understand, *compañeros*. Peach or apple?'

Although he'd never met the men before, Delta had gleaned on his previous visit to Portales Province that the Rivera clan was anything but close. Even then there were rumours of friction, sibling rivalry and paternal dominion. Subjecting the sons to a careful Joe Delta appraisal now, he reckoned he could understand one reason at least why the Rivera family ship sailed rough waters. He doubted he would be comfortable with these two as either brothers, sons or distant acquaintances. They struck him as jerks, but certainly not jerks to be taken lightly.

Bannerman had sized them up in much the same light, yet his manner reflected nothing but genial goodwill and easy-going charm. He appreciated the fact that Delta was smart enough to hold his tongue and mainly listen and nod. Lady Luck had handed them a golden opportunity to win the confidence of the enemy when Limpy had turned ugly, and he was determined to make the most of the opportunity to get to know the enemy.

These men were the sons of Rivera, and the *señor* was the abductor of Jordan's male child, a kidnapper and a man with a reputation for autocracy and much worse in the province of Portales.

So he allowed the two to impress him with their erudition, accepted their expressions of gratitude gracefully, and eventually got to steer the conversation away from the general to the particular when

71

Tomas gave him the opening he'd been waiting for.

'Does that cowboy have a grudge against you gentlemen?' he asked innocently.

'Durant?' Paulo sneered. 'He hates the whole world because he is nothing! It would be agreeable, would it not, that his wounds would infect and his leg would drop off his mangy body?'

'We didn't know you gents were in any way important,' Delta put in now. 'But when we saw a joker trying to murder you just because of a few kicks and punches, heck, we just had to chime in and worry about the consequences later. Right, pard?'

'It was nothing,' Bannerman said modestly. 'But having gotten to know you, we're double glad we were able to help out.' They were laying it on with a trowel now, and before the head waiter arrived with the bill they had got what they were after and what they had been hinting at throughout the meal. To show their gratitude properly, the brothers insisted they come out to the ranch and meet with their family.

As luck would have it, the *patrón* and *patrona* were holding a banquet tomorrow evening, and Señores Bannerman and Delta were hereby offically invited.

Piedra was growing sleepy yet made no move to close up or invite his last two customers to take their trade elsewhere. In light of what the cantina keeper had seen Gene Bannerman do in the ruckus with Durant, and naturally wary of a character like Delta, he was not going to do anything but grin and bear it as he held up his heavy head in his cupped hand, elbow on the bar and a cold cigarette pasted to his lower lip, too bushed to set it alight.

By sharp contrast his American clients seemed full of energy and talk as they worked on a bottle over by the poker layouts. Yet even half-awake Piedra was aware that their moods were quite different. The tall Bannerman appeared genial and relaxed while his companion was taut-faced and tense, quite different from his earlier swagger and good-natured banter.

Bannerman, savouring their luck and success with the brothers, was not much interested in whatever was griping his hard-drinking companion, but was destined to hear about it anyway.

'So they've invited us to break bread with them. Big deal. I mean, that might strike a big-noter like you just fine – showing the world you've got what it takes to smarm your way in just any old place you happen to lob. Born glad-handers like you are like that, I know. But hobnobbing with silvertails or greaser would-bes ain't my idea of a fine old time by any stretch. I've half a mind not to show out there tonight, if you want to know the truth.'

The liquor trickling down the back of Gene's throat was smooth and mellow. He felt the same way. He didn't want to involve himself in whatever was griping Delta but supposed he couldn't overlook the man's mood, for obvious reasons. They were working hand in hand, had agreed to do so before he freed the hardcase from Hondo City jail.

Delta had proved invaluable in selecting the best trails and keeping them clear of the trouble spots, the towns and those buzzards of the border, the

Rurales. Bannerman had to concede the man had conducted himself tolerably well since their arrival and had proven himself a solid back-up to have at your shoulder when things went wrong. But Delta was still Delta, he reflected. Meaning he was still a dangerous heller from the shady side of the street with a bad reputation with both guns and women who probably didn't give a rap for anybody living, maybe not even Jordan.

It seemed characteristic that the man should grow aggressive in his cups.

'We made a deal,' he reminded. 'You help me get this kid back and in return I'll tell them in Keylock that you busted me and got away, any old tale will do. That means if I say we go to the spread tomorrow, we go.'

'What's the point in either of us going? Look, Sir Lancelot or whatever your sister calls you, you are talking to the man who's been here before, who made a try at getting his hands on that kid and ended up losing four good men and was lucky to get back over the Rio with a healthy ass. What I'm saying is that when it comes time to make our play, being on kissing terms with Rivera or any of that crap won't be worth a plugged nickel.'

Delta leaned back and slapped both gunbutts loudly.

'This is the way, the only way. We're going to have to plan real good, likely recruit extra guns – no short-age of Rivera enemies down here – then take them at their weakest point and time, and be prepared to blow the living shit out of anybody and everybody who tries to stop us. There ain't no other way.'

Delta had been happy with the headway they'd made with the enemy earlier. But the later it got the more he reverted to type.

'There's always another way,' Gene insisted. 'An old axiom of battle, mister – know your enemy. I mean to get to know Rivera and study his set-up at first hand. We had a lucky break with the sons and we're going to capitalize on it, meaning we will show up tomorrow all neat and good-mannered and we will play the gringo businessmen and Mex lovers for all it's worth. And you will like it.'

No response. Delta didn't hold his liquor as well as he might. He paused to drain his glass then leaned an elbow on the table.

'All right, now we've cleared that up – what is really chewing on your liver? I know it's not hand-kissing rich *haciendados*. You love faking and conning and mixing with people with deep pockets who you might get to fleece. So what is it?'

Without a word the sullen hardcase jammed his hat on his head and weaved out into the night. Staring back through a window, he saw Bannerman shrug indifferently and pour himself a nightcap. His hand strayed to gunbutt and for just a moment twin spots of deep red showed in hazel eyes. Then he swore and jumped off the high porch to land in the deep dust of the plaza to walk away beneath the hazy amber glow of the flickering streetlamps.

He pulled off his hat again to allow the cool night air to cool his brain.

Joe Delta's make-up could be compared to a finely

crafted piece of Swiss clockwork – but with a cog missing. Mostly the machinery ticked over just fine and he was capable of doing just about anything he set his mind to, whether it be something illegal, generous, hair-raising or even admirable.

But mostly was not all the time, and when the snake stirred inside him and he decided he wanted someone's money, their woman or even their life, he was a different man. Tonight, with his reprieve from prison or gibbet fast fading in his mind, he was sore at Bannerman for any number of reasons, but one in particular. The man's prickly vanity and pride were affronted by the fact that Bannerman had been able to track him, had shot it out with him, jailed him then virtually gave him no option but to agree to ride down here with him where they both had a first-rate chance of getting killed.

Yet these were not the aspects of their unlikely partnership that had touched off his trigger temper this late night. This went deeper. Much deeper.

For during their two-hour session with the arrogant, college-educated and filthy rich Riveras, Bannerman had slotted smoothly in with the pair on a social and intellectual level that had him feeling almost like a clodhopper farmboy.

He realized that Bannerman was not only about the most formidable son of a bitch he'd ever tangled with, but a class above in every other way that counted, maybe even several classes. This new awareness was abrading the outlaw's towering vanity and he could be at his dangerous worst whenever that occurred. Whenever he suspected that another man might actually consider himself his superior, something lethal and unstoppable could take him over – could and had led to violence and even funerals in his chequered past.

He stopped on a corner to replace his hat, taking several deep breaths as he stared up at an old Aztec moon hanging in a dark sky. The liquor was wearing off and he was now warning himself not to do anything hasty or dumb, not for any boozy reason.

Sometimes he could manage to get that 'loose cog' working properly again by a pure act of will. But not always.

CHAPTER 6

LAIR OF THE ENEMY

Bannerman guided the blaze-faced black past the ruined mission on the return leg of his early-morning circuit of Morelos and its tranquil surrounds. And even though his mind was busy with other things he realized he knew what the ruins were from a conversation he'd had with an ancient scholar on the town square the previous day.

The Mission of San Miguel dated back to the 1700s when the Jesuits arrived from Spain and set up their schools which for many years enjoyed the reputation as the finest in all the Americas, north or south. But they failed to educate the Apaches who rose against this mission and destroyed it fifty years later, and in 1767 the Jesuits were expelled by order of Charles the Third of Spain, never to return.

Now only the *ricos* like the Riveras could afford to

send their offspring to the colleges in the south while the poor were left with their new religion and little more.

He smiled ironically. He realized his thinking was targeting the haves and sympathizing with the have-nots, as always. But travelling along this dusty Mexican road with the sun climbing over his shoulder and the day's first cheroot between his teeth, he could smell a whiff of hypocrisy in himself somewhere. True, this operation might be well-motivated, but when it came down to hard-edged reality, he knew there would most likely be bloodshed and maybe even killing before he got to carry his nephew across the Rio Bravo del Norte.

If he succeeded he would be doing something for his sister but certainly would not be improving anyone else's lot in this rich-poor, sad-happy land. The contrary, most likely, Bannerman, he told himself candidly.

He sighed. Sometimes youthful idealism had to take a battering in the reality of adult life. He'd come to terms with that long ago. Here, he knew, as in other like undertakings of his life, he would do what had to be done and fret about the cost at another time.

The big tree-lined square was crowded by the time he rode in and once again he found himself the cynosure of all eyes. In the thick shadow of the arcade a knot of men sporting straw sombreros gusted tobacco smoke into the clear morning air and followed the progress of the rider astride the big-barrelled black with white face and stockings. Bannerman rode ramrod erect with tailored twill pants tucked into his boots, full-sleeved cream shirt and flat-brimmed hat, sunlight winking from gunbutts and cartridge rims.

A man called something to him but he didn't hear. When he swung down at the hotel hitchrack, the loafers gathered there stared at him and started jabbering in Spanish. Then one came forward and pointed across the square.

'Señor, I think your amigo maybe in trouble, you know?'

By the time he reached the vacant lot between the drygoods store and the tortilla bakery, the rising cloud of dust pinpointed where the trouble was.

It was Delta slugging it out with three Americans. His 'partner' was bleeding, cursing and fighting dirty yet still managed to put up a commendable showing despite the odds. Disgustedly, Gene strode straight into the mêlée and had no difficulty in bringing it to a halt with just a few well chosen words, then dropped one hand to a gun handle.

It turned out Delta had started the ruckus with a powerfully built waddy from Zeke Cromwell's Texas Ranch over a woman – naturally, and Dewey Henry's friends had chimed in to support him.

He grabbed the weaving Delta by the shoulder and hauled him halfway across the lot out of earshot.

'Are you loco?' he hissed. 'You said yourself we might have to recruit from Cromwell's crew if we got in over our heads. Yet here you go brawling with them and getting them all stirred up and sore. Is this dumb or isn't it?'

Unrepentant but feeling all the better for a good dust-up, the other spat blood and dabbed at his mouth with a bandanna.

'Whatever you say, Mr Bannerman sir,' he said sarcastically, still breathing hard. 'You are the king pin and ramrod of this operation, sir.'

Bannerman slammed the man's shoulder with the heel of his hand, driving him back several yards. Delta's eyes flared dangerously, but Gene spoke over him as he started in cursing.

'I told you last night to straighten up, mister. Now I'm ordering. From here on in you are going to keep your nose clean or all bets are off. I'll turn you into the law here to await extradition back to Texas, and finish this job alone. I mean it. So, do you go patch up things with these men, then go get yourself smartened up for tonight, or do I take you on a one-way walk to the *calabozo*?'

He meant it. Delta could see it. He seemed almost genuine about it when he turned and walked across the lot and proffered his hand to Dewey Henry. The last a tolerably satisfied Bannerman saw of them, all four were heading for the Riata Cantina for a make-up drink.

'You're an unpredictable cuss,' opined Dewey Henry, rolling a durham one-handed. 'Try and kick a man's head off one minute, treatin' him to drinks the next.' He licked tobacco and paper into an even white cylinder and eyed it admiringly, a clear-eyed man with a quick and easy way of doing things. Shrewd.

'You always this way or only when you're in Mexico?'

'Guess I was born unpredictable,' confessed Delta with an affable smile. 'But then again, that *señorita* was shining up to me, not you.'

The Cromwell cowboy-gunhand torched his smoke into life and leaned against a sturdy porch support of the livery stables, squinting at the afternoon sun. A make-up drink had parlayed into a game of poker, a bowl of chilli and a stroll around the back streets, where hardcases like Henry felt more at home anyway.

The two hit it off, which suited Delta just fine. Henry was his kind of man, tough, cocky and game for anything. Not in his class with fists or a Colt, naturally. But he didn't rub a man up the wrong way as Bannerman did just by being Bannerman.

'Women!' Henry said philosophically. 'But I'll tell you something about that Catarina jade. She won't put out for you any more than she will for me. Ask me, she's an ice box. All over a man in company, then freezes up the minute you're alone with her.'

'They put out when I want them to put out,' Delta declared with a momentary scowl. Then he brushed back a handful of black curls and asked, 'What time you got?' Henry told him and he sighed. 'I'd best go take a tub and get duded up for the big bash out at Rivera's, I guess.'

'You don't sound too eager.'

Delta shrugged. 'I like my fun on the rough and ready side. I'm expecting to be bored rigid tonight.'

There came the rhythmic creaking of wheels. It was the wagons taking the miners out to the Casias

Canyon Mine, another Rivera operation which kept fifty men busy two shifts a day. The water wagon followed the two heavy transports, laying their dust before it could blow. The mules' harness glittered too brightly causing Henry to squint as he spoke.

'So, it's goin' on into the night, is it?'

'Far as I know.' Delta gave his lopsided grin. 'Why, thinking of gate-crashing?'

'Reckon not,' replied the other, electing to take him seriously. 'They are dung-eatin' maggots that Rivera outfit, don't you know, buddy. Take, grab, kick-ass. You name it and that Diego Rivera has done it and'll go on doin' it so long as he breathes. And they think they are so fine! Only for Cromwell this whole damn region would be totally under Rivera's thumb. We've fought the bastard every inch for over five years now. They've handed us some beatin's but we have cost them plenty more'n once too.'

Delta might have answered 'I know.' For the Rivera–Cromwell range war had been burning bright when he'd been here last. In recent time it appeared Texas Ranch had lifted some of Rivera's blood horses, and when San Cristobal struck back they put four Cromwell hands in the ground.

He took a longer, more critical look at his new friend in light of this knowledge, realizing that maybe it had been fortuitous his meeting up with hard-hating Dewey Henry this way. He was not sure if Bannerman really believed they might be driven to recruit men to help get their job done – him being the bighead he was. Delta believed he was more down to earth and practical in matters like this, and had the experience to back himself up.

'I got you figured as a hard man to kick around,' he declared. 'You and your riding buddies. Like your style. Mebbe we'll get together next time you're in town?'

'I'd admire to do that,' Henry responded with an answering grin. He nodded. 'Uh huh, I reckon we get along just fine.' He punched Delta's shoulder lightly, and winked. 'That's if we both keep away from Catarina, that is?'

'Might be an idea.'

They shook hands and Delta turned to go. 'Only hope they keep the liquor flowing out there tonight. I've a notion I'll need to stay half-cut to put up with all the high-faluting bullshit I expect to find floatin' around thick as buffalo dust.'

'Have fun,' the Cromwell man called after him, leaning lazily back against the roof support like a man too relaxed and comfortable to do anything but lean and dream. Yet the moment Delta disappeared, Dewey Henry darted inside the livery, threw his saddle across his bronc and quit town at a speed that left the water wagon driver cursing in his dust.

Gene Bannerman was the hit of the evening.

The *ranchero*'s guest list for such functions was selective and limited with the result that over time everyone got to know everyone else so well that the opulent social functions and get-togethers at San Cristobal, although eminently elegant, tended to be predictable and even boring.

Neither the family nor their *rico* guests were

renowned for making strangers feel welcome, except when they they happened to be people almost as important and superior as themselves. That night they were initially distant with the two Americano guests – invited without either the knowledge or approval of their father by the Rivera sons – although several of the younger women seemed sharply conscious of Bannerman right from the outset. But it was impossible not to socialize just a little, and it was not too long before the guests realized that the tall gringo talked, acted and possibly thought, just like themselves.

The tall Americano obviously had breeding and education it was decided, and once the barricades came down he became the centre of attention to the point where Diego Rivera hardly saw the point of maintaining his own critical aloofness any longer. He approached Gene to thank him personally for assisting his sons while he was conversing with the daughter of the Mexico City emissary. He didn't get very far. The couple had been discussing books and writers, and the girl insisted Señor Rivera listen while Señor Bannerman repeated a quotation he'd just cited from a history on King Arthur.

Bannerman demurred but the girl insisted.

'All right,' he said. 'It's a brief description of the knights of the round table and it goes, "This glorious company – the flower of men".'

The girl clapped her hands. 'Aren't they wonderful words, Señor Rivera. They could have been writing about your family, couldn't they?'

Deciding then and there that the stunning girl

from Mexico City might be a little sugary for his taste, Gene was excusing himself when he glanced up and saw them. Emerging from the massive double doorway which opened on to the vast stucco patio of the finest house he'd ever been in, was a young woman leading a boy of about eight or nine by the hand.

He stopped in his tracks. He knew he was staring but couldn't help it.

'Ahh, a servant with my youngest, Señor Bannerman. They make a handsome picture, do they not?'

This was an understatement.

The child, whom he instantly realized was Jordan's son, was dark-haired, clean-featured and shining-faced, quite the most exceptional looking boy he'd ever seen. Yet even though seeing his nephew for the first time, he couldn't keep his gaze from straying to the servant girl, the *niñera*, now leading the boy towards the lawns across the patio.

She was stunning. Tall and Indian-looking with bluish-black hair and high cheekbones, the girl was tall and graceful as a deer with slanted green eyes and summer-ripe lips, lush as peaches. The combination of the simple but elegant clothes she was wearing, and the dignity of her bearing combined to ensure that she looked like anything but a servant. In Bannerman's eyes she looked more like quality than any of the glossy, coiffed and gowned ladies of quality present.

'My son Matthew James,' Rivera introduced. 'My boy, this is Mr Gene Bannerman from Texas.'

They shook hands gravely and Gene felt an instant

and tremendous hit to the heart at the physical contact. At once he felt stunned, astonished, exhilarated. In the short space of one week he had found his long-lost sister, was now hunkering down before a handsome boy child with the Bannerman blood coursing through his young veins. Instantly he saw his own father in him, maybe a little of Aunt Martha, other Bannermans both living and dead.

Jordan's son. His nephew.

He shook his head slowly as emotion and understanding flooded his face. He was a rich and successful man, but a man alone. He'd known a hundred women but had never been in love so had never married. Parents gone, estranged from his only sibling, he'd regarded himself as an independent, possibly self-contained man who didn't seem to need the closeness and comfort other men found in wife and family.

But this child had his blood in his veins, and in the space of a heartbeat the blood tie had connected and would be there for life.

By the time he straightened and blinked at his surrounds he knew he'd undergone some great change. His gaze swept the scene and was amazed how it all seemed to have altered. Where before he'd seen elegant, handsome and cultivated people he now saw only aliens in jewels and fine linens whose dark Spanish looks seem to suggest something decaying and evil. The pretty women weren't that any more; the men had become enemies he may well have to kill in order to complete what had begun as a simple rescue operation such as he'd accomplished before, but had now become a sacred quest – a crusade.

He shook his head. The fog cleared. Control. He looked down. 'A pleasure to make your acquaintance, Matthew James. Ever been to Texas?'

'Never,' Rivera answered for him. '*Gracias*, Maria, you may go.'

'Wait,' Bannerman said, rising quickly. He needed something to divert him from the darkness that had gripped him. He extended a hand. 'Maria, is it? I'm Gene.'

The girl glanced quickly at Rivera. Protocol was plainly being challenged here. Rivera cleared his throat disapprovingly but Gene chose not to hear. He was still clinging to her hand. 'May I fetch you a drink, *señorita*?'

'*Por favor*, Señor Bannerman,' Rivera protested. 'I said Maria is a—'

'A lovely young lady without a drink, *señor*,' Bannerman cut in, almost tersely. His face was pale and there was a strange look in his eyes as he glanced again at the boy and felt the tingling in his hands and wrists, a familiar experience which usually prefaced violence or gunplay. 'If you'll excuse us, I'd like to get some refreshments for your son and Señorita Maria, and get to know them both a little better. I'm sure you have no objections?'

Rivera the aristo had plenty. But a small crowd had gathered round, smiling and nodding, and it didn't seem the time to voice them.

'Very well,' he said stiffly. He beckoned. 'Cody. Accompany my son, will you.' He looked at Gene.

'Señor Mears is Matthew James's personal guardian.' He shrugged resignedly. 'A necessity for a rich man's son. I'm sure you understand?'

Bannerman turned as the trim-bodied man in tailored leather jacket and snug-fitting black chinos threaded through the crowd. The moment he met the calculating impact of Cody Mears' cool grey gaze he had him fitted. Gunman. They had a certain look. There was an economy of motion about such men, a self-assurance, such as must have characterized the golden warriors of Camelot, he thought.

'I hear we owe you one, Bannerman.' The man's tone was impersonal. He didn't sound all that grateful. When Bannerman just stared, he added, 'The *señor*'s sons?'

'Oh, yeah. Well I—'

'I get paid to protect the *señor*'s family. Big money.'

Bannerman's expression remained blank. 'So I believe.'

'I guess you've heard of me then?'

'Not really. Should I have?'

'Cody Mears – Denver, Colorado?'

'Sorry.'

He knew the name, just wasn't about to admit it. He expected the man to tire of the mainly one-way conversation, but he didn't. Rivera's gunslinger had something he wanted to get across.

'When Señor Rivera needed someone to protect his child he searched all over until he heard about me. Sent a party all the way to Denver just to hire me. I told him to double the dough he was offering and we had a deal. So, now we know just who I am, who are you, Bannerman? I mean, really?'

The man's tone was edgy, challenging. Was he genuinely suspicious, or was it just the way he was?

He was saved replying when Maria spoke.

'I do think Matthew James would like some ice cream, *patrón*,' she suggested. Then added daringly, 'If you would like to accompany us, Señor Bannerman?'

He nodded to his host and the three moved away towards the tables beneath the trees together, the brow of Diego Rivera dark and thoughtful as he stared after them.

He found Delta at the buffet table with a wide-eyed blonde who seemed to be clinging to his every word. The man greeted Bannerman boisterously, made a fuss of the boy and ogled the maid. He then straightened to glare suspiciously at Mears as though recognizing another of his own lethal breed. But he was obviously in good spirits and didn't start anything, much to Bannerman's relief.

From there the evening flowed.

The sun was going down in a splendour of rose and gold as the *mozos* or servants began bringing the serious food out to load up the tables that had been set up across the patio. In lightning time every square inch of three of these tables pushed together was covered with delicious steaming things to eat.

Spread before them the guests found golden cheese decanted into capsules of the airiest crust. There were tissue-thin tortillas spread with a green sauce; chillis in walnut sauce. The centre dish was an enormous bowl of *mole negro*, with its texture of boiling chocolate throwing off cinnamon steam from floated tender chunks of turkey, peanuts, pecans, almonds, spare ribs and raisins.

The beaming chef dealt out hands of tortillas as though they were rounded playing cards. Even the most elegant and refined couldn't help but lean forward, get serious and attack the repast the way it was intended – full-on and forget the etiquette.

Seated here amongst all this largesse and watching the light fade across miles and miles of rich cattle graze, a now-calm Bannerman alternately chatted or listened to a knowledgeable old don fill out his skimpy knowledge of the family and their kingdom. Seemed Rivera's antecedents had employed highly questionable legal tactics and quite a deal of both bribery and coercion in order to acquire the combined grants of a dozen small landholders a century earlier, with each successor adding to the ranch until it now occupied ten leagues, almost 45,000 acres.

One third of that vast landscape was uninhabitable chaparral of the sierras, but the flatland, rich with *alfilerilla* and other excellent grasses and studded lavishly with acorn-bearing oaks, supported a herd the size of which would make all but the very largest Texas ranches appear modest by comparison.

Bannerman was interested in all this but more so in studying this family in relaxed mode. Despite his lavish trappings, he found he didn't really envy Rivera as he found himself studying *el patrón* from a short distance.

Diego was a handsome and virile looking man of

fifty but his dowdy wife appeared infinitely older. The couple had lost their two eldest sons in the range wars, while the survivors, Paulo and Tomas, just didn't appear the kind who'd bring you comfort and pleasure in your maturing years.

There was something palpably snaky about the junior Riveras who seemed to prefer one another's company, except when mingling with several other pampered looking young men of their own status away from the main throng.

The entire hacienda, zoo, orchards and surrounds were guarded by pacing figures with big hats and large guns, a fact not lost on the man who might soon have to face the challenge of cracking the heavy security if he were to succeed in rescuing his nephew.

And the governor had a special bodyguard just for his son – the child he'd stolen from Gene's sister.

This puzzled the American as he scoffed *frijoles rancheros* and washed them down with the ranch's own excellent red.

To him it didn't figure that, after all this time, Rivera should fear any further attempt from the mother to retrieve her child. Jordan had made her desperate play years ago, had failed, and taken to the drink. Rivera would know this, know she no longer posed any threat.

Yet if such was the case, then why Cody Mears?

His duty was clear. Concentrate on the American gunpacker for the moment and assess just how much of a hazard he might pose to his plans. Simple.

So why didn't he do this right away while he had the chance?

The answer was Matthew James and his servant-cum-*niñera*, Maria.

His new-found personal involvement set aside, Bannerman knew he'd honestly never encountered a child so captivating or a woman so lovely before. The boy stunned him. Matthew James, with his clear eyes and precocious intelligence, might have been Gene Bannerman thirty years ago. The child appeared to respond warmly to him, and he could now fully understand the years of heartbreak his sister had gone through after he was taken from her, could even understand the bottle and the Crib Street address.

He made a small joke to the child and both laughed, Matthew James and Maria. The dusk was coming down as the Chinese lanterns slung from the trees were lighted, and it was a rare moment of beauty and peace for a man who had come a long way to the tranquillity of this place, most probably for all time.

Yet the self-styled troubleshooter, who still clung to ideals of a long-gone time, was to actually find an hour or two of rare peace and pleasure spent mostly in the company of the boy and his nurse, until the incident.

He was hardly surprised when a fat man in ruffled shirtfront and silver-trimmed charro pants was pushed backwards into a fountain, and, sure enough, there was Delta with glass in hand challenging the servants who came rushing up to investigate.

'He had it coming and he got it, gents,' the hard-case stated loudly. 'So don't go getting all excited.

He's a fat shoat who hates Americans and made a grab at my girl. End of story.'

Bannerman excused himself and hurried across to the fountain just as Rivera and his sons appeared upon the patio.

'It's all right,' he called, taking Delta by the arm. 'My friend is just leaving.' Then under his breath, 'Right – pardner?'

Delta shook himself loose, drunk and aggressive.

'Listen to Mr Brown-nose,' he snorted. 'Well, you can soft-soap these greaseballs all you want, Bannerman, but Joe Delta's not the suck-up kind—'

He broke off as Bannerman reefed his arm up behind his back and marched him for the stables. Delta was white with fury by the time they got there but Gene was none too serene himself. He shoved the hardcase away from him, up against the stables wall, then stood back a pace with hands on hips.

'You are fouling things up and I'm not about to let that happen, mister,' he said. 'So get gone, get sober and forget any notions about taking me on as you could not do it sober and sure as shooting can't do it drunk.' He jerked a thumb in the direction of the trail. '*Vamanos!*'

Delta was drunk, but not suicidally so. He wouldn't take this further. It was a disgruntled and cussing American guest who forked his bronc to go storming away across Rivera's gravelled driveway minutes later. But he did leave, which was all Bannerman cared about at the moment. As he turned to return to the party a figure detached from a cluster of flower trees

94

and he found himself confronting Mears again.

The men stood ten feet apart sizing one another up. Then Gene said evenly, 'Trouble's over. He's gone.'

'I'm not interested in any two-bit guntipper, if that's what he is, Bannerman. It's you that's got me puzzled.'

'Oh?' His tone was level. 'How so?'

'Because I can't seem to read your brand, is why.'

'Nothing complicated about me. I'm just another Yankee businessman looking for ways of making Mexican money.'

'And a guntipper.'

Bannerman's dark brows lifted quizzically. 'What makes you say that?'

'This,' replied the bodyguard, tapping the side of his nose with a forefinger. 'When you've been around the traps as long as me you get so you can pick a gelding from a stud on sight.' He stepped closer. He was not as tall as Bannerman but was lean, athletic and hard looking. Their eyes locked. 'I sure hope I don't have any trouble with you, Texan. Something about you just doesn't hit me right somehow. Now I don't give a damn if you're here to chase women, rob a bank or start up your own ranchero . . . couldn't care less. But just understand this: if you so much as spit on Rivera dirt or interfere with any of the people I'm paid to look out for, I'd blow you out of your boots in the blink of an eye and worry about dottin' the i's and crossin' the t's on the death certificate later. I'd like you to get that real clear in your mind.'

'Seems clear enough.'

'And just one more thing. Maria seems to be taking a shine to you and—'

'Let me guess. You want me to keep clear of her too?'

'You catch on quick.'

'Open a vein.'

Mears' eyes flared. 'What?'

'Nobody tells me what to do, mister, especially no tenth-rate guntipper with a big mouth and bad manners. As for Maria, if I choose to make a friend of her I'll do it and you can go bite your ass for mine. Got that clear, small-time?'

They stood face to face in total silence for what seemed a long time, playing the eye game. Weighing up each other's machismo. Neither really wanting to take it further, yet neither prepared to be first to back down, everyone else forgotten.

Until they were diverted by the sudden sound of racing hoofbeats from the south, the blast of a gunshot followed by a wild cry:

'Señor Rivera! Fire in the sky at the basin!'

Bannerman and Mears rushed from beneath the heavy trees into the open to sight the outrider galloping right up to the lawns, waving his hat and shouting. To the south beyond the low line of near hills, an orange light was climbing into the sky.

'What the hell. . . ? Gene gasped.

'Jiminez Basin where our married workers and their families live!' Mears yelled, already running for the stables. 'Could be Cromwell, but it's bad trouble for sure!'

The tall Americano was already running for the stables.

Families and children at risk? There was no way Gene Bannerman would turn his back on that.

CHAPTER 7

'DEATH TO THE GRINGO!'

There were adobes already in ruins and several outbuildings well ablaze by the time the San Cristobal party topped out the trail which curved down into the tight little wooded basin some ten minutes later. The Riveras and Mears were ready to ride directly down, but Bannerman halted them when he insisted they should parley first and go fire-fighting later.

Diego Rivera heeled across to the tall Texan with a curse. 'Señor, you are my guest and perhaps you do not understand. But there are women and children down there in danger and—'

'As far as I can see,' Gene shot back, pointing down, 'the villagers are doing a good job of fighting the flames themselves, and they don't seem in immediate danger.'

'We've still got to go help them, damnit!' snarled Cody Mears, trying to hold his nervous mare.

But Bannerman shook his head firmly and swept a long left arm toward the eastern rim where a snarl of wind-shapened rocks and boulders loomed above the smoking basin.

'I saw something or somebody moving over there as we came over the rise,' he announced. 'I smell a rat, and a king-sized one. Seems to me if someone wanted to set up an ambuscade they could do worse than torch a few buildings then set up a shooting gallery from those boulders. And didn't you mention Cromwell back at headquarters, Mears?'

The horsemen traded stares. Then a *vaquero* hollered, '*Patrón*. I think I too see something over yonder now ... the moonlight on the gun barrel mebbe?'

The party grew quieter now as they switched attention from the scene below to the eastern rim. They started at the sound of a running horse, and the solitary rider who came highballing up over the rim behind them found himself confronted by a battery of guns as he first slowed, then dragged his hard-blowing horse to a halt mid-trail.

Joe Delta looked wide-eyed and stone sober as he jerked off his hat to identify himself. 'Saw the sky, figured you had troubles, *amigos*. What's going on, Bannerman?'

'A set-up is my guess,' Gene replied. Then to Rivera, 'They say you have plenty of enemies, *señor*—'

'*Madre*! It could be Cromwell!' Rivera barked,

glancing at Mears. His face tightened as he brandished a silver-plated pistol. 'All follow me. *Arriba, arriba!*'

Bannerman, Mears and Delta were riding in the middle of the pack as Rivera led the cavalcade on the semi-circular route around the basin rim, horsemen cutting between the trees and shouting to one another to keep up their courage on either side.

He would have done it differently had he been in charge, Bannerman reflected as he lifted the white-blazed black over a deadfall. Circling round behind the rocks where the timber was thicker, then come up on anyone skulking amongst the boulders, would have been his plan of attack.

Too late for that now.

The storming volley which suddenly erupted from the rocks swept a scythe of lead through the leading riders. Men and mounts were going down in pandemonium as Bannerman cut his horse hard left with a vicious jerk on the reins. As his tall figure went plunging into the oaks, the most gunwise pair amongst the bunch, Delta and Mears, came spurring after him, Mears sliding down the off-side of his racing horse Indian-style as a shot slammed and the slug sang thinly from a rock close by.

Then the trio were in the deeper timber and swinging south again. With naked guns in hand they ducked low-reaching limbs and heard horses starting up directly ahead and higher up.

'They are hightailing!' yelled Delta who'd lost his hat and was grinning with the excitement of it. 'If we keep going straight instead of cutting back towards the rocks, we can cut them off.'

So it played out.

As the oaks thinned and Mears led the way across a low, lumpy ridge, the enemy hove into sight, some five or six men in American rig riding hoofs and heels away from the rocks where gunflashes were still flaring.

'Cromwell!' Mears bawled, and cut loose at a low-crouching rider scorching over the shaley ground atop a long-legged buckskin.

He didn't miss. The buckskin stood on its nose and the screaming rider was silhouetted against the sky as he was hurled high to come down brutally hard, head-first into a wagon-sized boulder that didn't give an inch.

Within seconds a fierce fire-fight had erupted east of the rocks where in the first handful of moments the six gun superiority of the ranch trio manifested itself with lethal impact. Men were dropping or sagging in their saddles when Gene suddenly let out a warning yell. In an instant the three found themselves forced on to the defensive as the second half of the ambusher pack got their mounts beneath them and came driving in on them triggering rifles from hip level and laying the fire down hot and heavy.

Only quick thinking and lightning reflexes saved Cody Mears as his horse collapsed beneath him and lead slashed the grass all about him as he hit the ground running. Cutting behind the downed horse, Delta bawled at the running man then dropped a long arm as he thundered abreast. Mears grabbed hold of it, almost jerking Delta from his saddle.

Somehow they managed to keep going as Bannerman cut about in a tight little circle to fan a Colt full of storming lead at the onrushing riders, was rewarded as a figure tumbled backwards over his mount's bouncing rump with a gurgling cry then rolled ten feet and lay still.

Moments later the trio was in amongst the oaks leaving behind them an open line of retreat for the ambushers who were gone in a storm of hoofbeats and a roil of dust, taking their wounded with them but leaving their dead behind.

Five dead, all identified as Texas Ranch hands and gunsharks on the Cromwell payroll. They had killed two San Cristobal *vaqueros*, wounded three more and burned several adobes and half a dozen outbuildings below.

In the dazed and bloody aftermath, Diego Rivera vowed bloody retaliation. And who could blame him? The *ranchero*'s wrath was in no way diminished when he realized later that, in the rush and confusion, he had not realized that his sons had not shown up at Jiminez Basin until it was all over.

Cody Mears turned out for breakfast in the family's enormous dining room with a wrenched left arm neatly encased in a black calico sling. Delta, already seated at the long oaken table with Bannerman, the Riveras and their sullen sons, with Maria assisting with the serving, was smoking and drinking coffee as he furnished an amusing-sounding account of what had in actuality been a savage and murderous foray. He boasted a bullet burn on his left forearm which

102

he had not been aware of until well after the gunsmoke blew away.

Bannerman had emerged unscathed, yet was sober and reserved as he stared at the plate of *frijoles* placed before him. When he glanced up at Maria he saw her face showing pale and drawn by the light filtering through the great ceiling-high windows. The atmosphere was taut despite Delta's gabby attempts to lighten things. The boy was not present. Rivera did not wish to worry his youngest with what he had to say this San Cristobal morning.

The authorities had been alerted regarding the Texas Ranch attack, and a posse comprising riders from both Morelos and the San Cristobal had already stormed Cromwell's stronghold, only to find it deserted with the rancher having fled to the hills. This satisfied Rivera for the moment yet his mood was still vicious as he ignored his plate and drew hungrily on a cigar. He glared at Paulo and Tomas who had prudently taken their places at the far end of the table.

That Señor Rivera was disappointed in his two sons would appear to be an understatement. He was closer to disgusted. He was even closer still to total fury. When he finally got started, he handed sullen Paulo and pale Tomas the dressing down of their young lives as the *frijoles* got cold and even Delta had difficulty maintaining his determined air of droll amusement.

The sons were unworthy to bear the name Rivera, the father accused. He had given them every opportunity to prove themselves worthy of their great heritage, yet they continued to fail him. Was it any wonder that, due to their manifest shortcomings and failures, the *patrón* had been driven to reclaiming their half-brother – the outcome of a dalliance Rivera had openly admitted to long since – in the desperate hope that when his time came there might be at least one product of his loins with the character and the capacity to succeed him?

There was more, much more.

Eventually Bannerman had heard enough. He excused himself despite Rivera's reproving glare, and quit the room. Soon Mears and Delta also found reasons for not wishing to sit in on the family blood-letting, and the Texans made their way for the stables.

They were readying their horses when Mears abruptly appeared in the double doorway.

The earlier friction between Bannerman, Mears and Delta appeared to have been temporarily forgotten in the aftermath of dangers shared and the impressive combination they'd exhibited during the gun battle. They'd faced death together and now some fragile sense of brotherhood prevailed.

'Obliged,' Mears stated.

'You're welcome,' said Delta. 'So, what'll happen next, you figure?'

The gunman shrugged.

'Rivera is too sore at the sons to be able to concentrate on Cromwell right now, I guess.' He glanced back at the *hacienda* over his shoulder. 'Seems pretty obvious that that mangy Texican decided to take advantage of the banquet to set up an ambush and maybe do what he's been trying to do for years – namely put Rivera under and take over this land which he claims doesn't legally belong to the family anyway.'

'Well, he has surely done himself in now,' commented Gene, leading the black out into the sun-filled yard.

'Sure has. He's never gone this far before and he'll swing for sure when he is caught.'

'Thought you'd be out hunting for him,' remarked Delta as he joined them outside. 'I mean, you do get paid big money to watch-dog this place, don't you?'

'My job's here,' Mears said distantly.

'Protecting the boy?' Bannerman queried.

'Sure.'

'From what?'

'You saw last night.'

'So,' Bannerman pressed, 'you're saying your job is to guard Matthew James against outsiders?'

'Who else?' Mears' features were blank.

Bannerman glanced pointedly towards the house. 'I thought you might tell us.'

They heard laughter and Matthew James rounded a corner of the great house with Maria giving chase. Bannerman stood silent and motionless, watching woman and child, his thoughts wandering, features inscrutable.

His look drew a warning from Mears. 'Sooner or later she will come round to me, Bannerman. I know that. You should know it too.'

But Gene was already moving off to greet the boy

with a smile. At that moment, Matthew James struck him even more forcibly than before as a total innocent amidst evil and danger, most of it only sensed despite last night's gun hell. He wanted to grab up the kid and tote him back to Texas right now, dreading what delay might bring.

He eyed Maria, and her lips barely moved as she whispered. 'I shall be in Morelos tomorrow night.' And without giving him time to be sure if he had really heard these words or not, took the boy by the hand and led him off towards the gardens and the zoo.

The tall gringo had much to occupy his mind on the ride back to Morelos.

She asked bluntly, 'What is the real reason you came to Morelos?'

Bannerman leaned back in his restaurant chair with a frown. He was immaculate in freshly pressed shirt and suiting. He was shaved and sober and had paid an urchin five centavos to coax the best shine from his blood-coloured boots and gunrig. He might deny it, yet knew he had gone to extra pains to make himself presentable that evening, had been curiously nervous about seeing Maria alone and away from the oppressive atmosphere of San Cristobal.

Very plainly, she had not been anticipating their meeting with anything like his degree of pleasure.

'Pardon?' he murmured.

They were seated in the front window of the best eatery on the square. In the dusk sky, tiny bats circled above the church spire while a prostitute solicited from the wide steps below, a casual combination between the spiritual and the temporal in the village of Morelos.

Already the belles were promenading in their starched blouses and brightly coloured skirts for the men, who, both young and old, gathered in knots along the walks at this time every evening.

Romance was in the air here but not at table two in the dining-room overlooking the square, apparently.

But surely there was no logical reason why it should be? Gene Bannerman reflected as he gazed across damask cloth, bottle, glasses, single rose and candle into the most striking face he'd ever seen. For he was still, after all, virtually a total stranger. Apart from that he was also a man who had come to this place quite ready to lie, deceive and yes, even kill if necessary in order to abduct from her care a child whom Maria obviously adored.

Wouldn't anyone be six kinds of a fool to trust someone like him?

'I don't understand your question,' he parried, unfolding his napkin.

'You are not really a man of commerce, are you?'

'Why do you say that?'

'The gun battle ... what you did. And Señor Mears also says you may be something very different, an outlaw perhaps, or perhaps a *pistolero*.'

There was irony here, mused Bannerman. Had he the time and desire he could easily have it confirmed that he actually was indeed a large landholder and dealer in land, stock and transport in Texas.

But of course, neither could he deny that he was indeed 'something different'. He was a man who pursued causes, who had never quite outgrown a powerful belief in the ethic of the strong assisting the weak. A fallible, latter day crusader who sometimes killed people and was prepared to lie and cheat all in the name of something called idealism.

'So, Mears said that?' he parried. 'Understandable, isn't it?'

'Why do you say that, *señor*?'

'Gene, *por favor*.' He smiled. 'He's attracted to you and thinks I might be also,' he stated. 'Naturally he'd paint me black as he can. But now you mention Mears I must say I'm very interested in that pilgrim. You just asked me why am I here in Morelos. Might I ask you why Cody Mears is at San Cristobal?'

'To protect Matthew James, of course.'

'From whom?'

'From those who might seek to harm him.'

The man came to wait upon them. Bannerman ordered for them both, even though she insisted she wasn't hungry. They were sampling the wine and about to resume their conversation when he spotted the girl from the cantina approaching along the wide walk with Joe Delta.

Delta was drunk. Again. Their rapprochement following their return to town had not lasted. Gene was fast losing confidence in Jordan's 'friend'. Delta was slipping back into character, living noisily and carelessly and primed for trouble.

He figured it typical of the man that he should continue to pursue the Riata girl, Catarina, when she

108

had made it perfectly clear he was simply not her type. That guntipper was the breed that liked to cut against the grain, brace the odds. A woman who took a shine to him right off would bore him witless. Delta was holding the scowling *señorita* by her little finger when he happened to glance up at the window. He immediately raised his hand and employed forefinger and thumb to form a circle in a gesture interpreted in international sign language as ' everything OK and coming up roses'.

'Your *amigo*,' Maria murmured as the couple disappeared. 'He also is a strange one.'

'Why did you come to town to see me, Maria?'

The soup arrived and she stared down at it for a long moment before finally raising slanted green eyes which looked almost turquoise in the candlelight.

'I fear for the child,' she said suddenly. 'I desperately need help and did not know who I could turn to or who I could trust – but a stranger.'

He thrust his bowl away.

'You can trust me,' he said, and meant it. He was ready to protect Matthew James with his life and sensed that in this regard at least they had common cause. 'What is it you fear? Rivera's enemies, is it? There seems to be no shortage of them judging by that attack.'

Maria inhaled a deep breath and looked out. 'I fear his brothers.'

Bannerman went still. The waiter approached but he waved him away. He rested his elbows on the tablecloth.

'Tell me why,' he ordered.

What she revealed over the following minutes slotted so neatly in with what Bannerman had already seen, sensed and perhaps half suspected, that he reproached himself for not having drawn the same conclusions himself. He quickly understood where her concerns were rooted as she began to talk slowly, deliberately and with intense concentration.

Diego Rivera all but despised his sons, and they plainly resented, or perhaps even hated him, she insisted – something that hardly came as a surprise to her listener. The *patrón* had exposed himself to public ridicule and moral condemnation by publicly admitting to the illicit affair responsible for the son and heir whom he had suddenly produced from his past and then proceeded to install as a full member of the family whether his offended wife or jealous sons could accept it or not.

In the eyes of Maria, the objective of the *ranchero*'s blatant actions involving the boy, and his attitude towards him, were glaringly apparent. He was grooming Matthew James to take over one day, which meant Paulo and Tomas, although the senior sons, would be relegated perhaps even as low as the poor relation status.

Then she spelled out her summation of the situation in simple halting words:

'Cody Mears' job is to protect Matthew James at home, and I believe he has been told to protect him from his stepbrothers. I fear Paulo and Tomas would harm the child, perhaps even kill him. You see, Paulo desires me and I have been able to coax things out of him that both warn and frighten me. I fear that so deep is their hatred of their father and their humiliation in having a mere child esteemed higher, they may harm the boy and possibly also Señor Rivera as well in order to seize the land which they regard as their own birthright, nobody else's. There, I have said it and can not take it back.'

The meal arrived. He insisted they both eat despite the sudden sense of urgency gripping him now. There had been upheaval on the ranch; an enemy attack, death and bloodshed. It seemed quite possible that the brothers might decide to take advantage of such a volatile situation to strike, which in turn suggested they mightn't have much time left.

But a good meal and company couldn't but help him get his thoughts straight.

They were talking soberly over coffee and wine when the sound of raised voices from the square attracted their attention. A number of villagers were gesticulating and shouting angrily, and when the curious waiter flung a window open, Gene heard the words '*gringo!*' and 'rape!' amongst the babble. When the mob sighted him and began pointing and shouting, he guessed who the 'gringo' in question might be. Then a man shouted, 'You sit there like the don while your *segundo* goes crazy. All *gringos* are the same. Death to the *gringos!*'

Bannerman rose calmly and dropped money on to the table.

'Sorry, but I've got to settle this if I can. How can I contact you?'

She told him, and he went striding for the doors.

Someone hurled a rock as he started across the plaza, making for the Riata Cantina. He broke into a run as the church belfry creaked once then began tolling its iron song.

CHAPTER 8

RIOT NIGHT

Bannerman could hear the rising murmur of the crowd echoing through the warren of side streets, alleys and vacant lots reaching away from the rear of the Riata. He had no notion where Delta might be by this time, but gauged by the clamour the mob was making that they did not have him as yet. They held hard and fast views on matters such as rape south of the border, as Delta was most likely aware by this.

But would the man care?

The Texan hardcase was a volatile and many-sided mix of good and bad, mostly bad. But one accusation that could not be levelled was that he lacked guts, bravado and a certain damn-you-to-hell panache. He'd boasted to Bannerman he would bed that woman, and if Morelos' angry mood now was anything to go by, he'd succeeded – whether she'd been willing or otherwise.

'Damn fool!' he muttered, and wondered yet

again if the gamble he'd taken in hauling the hell-raiser south would prove his smartest move or the dumbest.

He swung down the wide street half a block from the gaudy lights of the Riata where the front porch was now crammed with drinkers and passers-by who might figure it to be safer to follow the manhunt from a safe distance than risk getting involved. Smart citizens. He may have done so himself, if it wasn't for Jordan. He sensed Delta meant a great deal to his sister, although doubted if her feelings for him were returned. Still, he felt some sense of refracted responsibility and didn't want to see the crazy bastard hauled up a tree like a dog even if he was guilty.

There was no way he could guarantee he mightn't find himself in desperate need of Delta and his lightning gun before this Mexican hoe-down was over.

He was travelling at the half-run now, right hand on gunbutt, hearing his name again now as stragglers spotted his tall figure. He turned into the long crooked street that ran behind the cantina and continued on for half a block to the empty lot in back of the courthouse and jailhouse compound. Now he heard the voice of the mob rise sharply. They had surged back up Candido Real into the next block where they were surrounding an old barn, brandishing G brands and lanterns and screaming for the '*gringo* rapist's' filthy blood.

Then, suddenly: 'That is him! Bannerman. Hey, where is your *amigo, gringo*? Come, you must know! Is he at the barn, *capón*?'

The mob was wheeling towards him, faces flooded

in sepia hue from the torches. Ugly faces, twisted faces, righteous faces. They wanted action, any kind of action would do. Bannerman determinedly left his guns in leather. There was enough poison in the air tonight without his adding some angry, innocent blood to the stink.

He swung about to go loping down yet another squalid laneway angling back to the square. Several men came after him, but halted when he propped, faced them and slapped a hand noisily to gun handle.

This mob was mad, but who had ever seen any mob with nerve?

The town of Morelos knew every detail of last night's murderous gun battle at Jiminez Basin in which the tall Americano and his low-life amigo had graphically demonstrated just how deadly dangerous they were. They would still attack, of course, but not before they had another twenty or thirty *compañeros* at their side. Home-grown heroes had always been thin on the ground in Morelos, the principal reason why Diego Rivera dominated them so easily.

The uproar from the barn was fading behind Delta as he legged it along this narrow, unlighted street, hugging the decaying buildings close. When he caught a backward glimpse of her workplace, the cantina, his reckless grin dissolved into hard, tight creases.

That whore! He'd warned uppity Catarina not to yell but she'd yelled like bloody murder. You'd think she was a goddamn virgin who'd never had it before, let alone experienced the rare thrill of him allowing her to pretend he was taking her by force – when in reality she was taking him. Like she hadn't liked it, yet he knew she had. Then the screaming. That double-crossing jade! She had better find some swell place to hide from him after he shoe-horned his way out of this scrape, as he knew he would. He was ready to stack up corpses like cord wood if that was what it took. He was running loose and wolf-dog free and no greaser town would put a noose around Joe Delta's lucky neck.

Better towns had tried.

He waited in darkness until the street ahead lay empty, then darted across. He almost fell over a drunk sprawled close to the tall building, and tensed over him, gun arm ready to strike. But a drunken snore reassured him, and he breathed a little easier, warily slower now as he moved on.

The street to the livery was blocked by a bunch of men with lanterns. Delta pressed his back against a wall, listening to the hooting and hollering of the mob still clustered around the barn. The morons! He'd gone in there and straight out the back ten minutes earlier. They couldn't find a skunk in their own moustache.

He jumped a foot when a revolver roared quite close, then ducked as a bullet whammed into the wall by his head.

'It is heem!'

The hidden shooter suffered either from an underpowered larynx, or else was so scared his throat was closing over.

Recklessly, venomously, Delta let loose with three crashing shots, great gushes of purple smoke and yellow flame lighting up the dark place like day.

Then he bolted as angry voices screamed. 'Back here! Bring the ropes!'

Seemed to him once a man got himself a bad name every broken-winded, ragged-assed dingle-dodie under the sun just couldn't wait to drag your boots off the ground at the hurting end of a rope then laugh their ugly Mex heads off when your tongue shot out like you'd just backed bare-assed into a red-hot stove.

His pounding steps carried him to the square where he realized he was just a few doors down from the jailhouse. The lousy town was alive with danger by this, and suddenly Joe Delta knew what he was going to do.

'Get out of my way!' Bannerman barked at the three figures who suddenly loomed before him out of the darkness. They stopped, stared, recognized him and one began to yell. Three long strides carried him to the man, whom he swatted clear out of his sandals with a whack of gunbarrel he would feel for a month. The second figure dropped his lantern and the other bleated like a sheep.

'Just shut up, get off the streets and get home!' he barked. 'Or maybe you'd like a dose of what I handed Cromwell last night? He had notions he couldn't live up to just like you losers.'

He won that one. The towners were more scared of him in his present frame of mind than they were

117

of missing out on a chance to witness a good lynch-
ing.

He strode on, cursing Delta, cursing the mob but
mainly cursing the law. Where were they when
needed? He was on his way to find out.

What he found at the long squat jailhouse adja-
cent to the courthouse were locked doors and shades
drawn, which was more or less just what he expected.
For the Morelos law force was merely a token presence here; they were puppets of the real power, the
regional governor. But tonight he was determined
they'd remember they were lawmen, and act like it.

He would insist. He was the man with the gun.

Leaping up the steps he crashed his gunbutt
violently into the doorboards.

'*Teniente*! Open up! Get your men out here and
stop this riot before it gets out of hand.' He punished
the door again. 'You hear me? This is Gene
Bannerman!' Then he added for extra impact,
'Governor Rivera's friend. I demand you put a stop
to this and get—'

He broke off as a round Judas window in the
mahogany door slid open and a bright eye stared
out.

'Well I do declare it is my best buddy, old Noble
Boots himself,' came an all too familiar voice. 'All
right Deputy Tortilla, draw your bolt and let the man
in. This is getting to be quite a party.'

It was Delta.

Bannerman experienced both anger and relief as
he stepped inside to see the cocky figure lounging
against the desk, empty-handed, hands on hips and

flashing that quick grin that could mean anything or nothing. Also present in the big front room of the jailhouse were the fat *teniente* and two scrawny, trembling deputies. The fifth man was hatchet-jawed Dewey Henry from Zeke Cromwell's ranch looking almost as cocky and drunken as his new 'buddy', Joe.

Slowly Gene housed his gun. He was listening for mob sounds, but it seemed he had not been seen entering the building. In the distance, someone screamed and a gun barked twice.

'I should put a bullet through you,' he panted.

'You can try it, Mr Big. We're both carrying, and it's a free country.'

Bannerman could tell exactly where Delta's thinking was taking him. He'd raised hell, gotten away with it thus far, now had a gun buddy to back him, was plainly ready to crash or crash through. They would not take Delta alive, that was plain. If needs be the man would fight him, and in his current mood, with his brain fizzing with liquor and excitement might quite easily kill him.

'Did you do it?' he demanded.

'Told you I'd have her.'

Gene nodded. 'What happened here, Sheriff?'

The fat *teniente* groaned. 'He came to the door and offered to give himself up, but when we admit him he has the guns and demands the protection of the *calabozo*.'

'And this other one?'

'Henry has been in the cells two days for shooting at one of my deputies. Your evil *compañero* forced us to release him.'

'And arm him, don't forget,' smirked Dewey Henry, hitching up his gunbelt. 'Well met, wouldn't you say, Joey?'

Delta cocked his head. 'Could be the fun and games committee might show up here any minute,' he speculated soberly. 'If they'd found me here I was ready to feed them bits and pieces of lawmen until they let me quit town. But that was before you showed up, Texas. This is what you call a real lucky break. You might not be much of a saddle pard or much else, Bannerman, but you could talk milk into creamy butter, I swear.' He jerked his head towards the front. 'Want to make a try at sweet-talking them the hell away from here? Or do I take out the Bowie and start in lopping off ears?'

For the time he stood motionless feeling the drive and conviction draining out of him, like blood, Gene Bannerman was giving himself some real hell.

No longer ready to find excuses, he knew the decision he'd made to take advantage of Delta's involvement with his sister to recruit him had been a total mistake. He should have realized after an attack on a woman had led him to chase the wild man to Railroad City that a leopard couldn't change its spots – that the Texan would revert to type.

He knew where the child was, had ingratiated himself with Rivera, but certainly was no closer to rescuing Matthew James now than when he'd swum the Rio. And tonight, instead of taking advantage of Maria's visit to maybe formulate some plan of action, here he was forted up with the man seen by others as his pard, with an angry mob on the ran-tan outside.

But then something stirred in him, and he recognized it for what it was. It was the faith he'd always had in the notions of honour, courage and chivalry – the Camelot ideal. Others might think such principles superficial or even artificial, but they'd supported and expanded Gene Bannerman's whole way of living for twenty years. He would rather be accused of following an outmoded ideal than be a rakehell like Delta or a tyrant like Diego Rivera.

His shoulders straightened and the moment of weakness was gone as he turned from the *teniente* to confront the Texan.

'All right, here's the deal,' he announced. 'I want you gone, pilgrim. I reckon the *teniente* won't object to seeing you off, when the alternative could be seeing that mob rip his jail apart to get at you. I made a mistake thinking your connection with Jordan might guarantee your loyalty down here. You are scum, and scum will always rise to the s—'

'Look, before you get right back up on your high and mighty horse – pardner,' Delta said heatedly. 'Just remember I got you here without a hitch. I played straight with you. And you could easy have got yourself killed in that shoot-out on the spread without yours truly, and we both know it.'

Bannerman hesitated. He knew this to be true. But one thing did not outweigh the other.

'*Teniente*,' he demanded, 'will you agree to let him go if I give you my word he'll go and not come back?'

The fat lawman was sweating a freshet. Prior to Bannerman's arrival he'd found himself unarmed and terrified in the hands of a frightening man. He couldn't nod quickly enough. Just as quickly, Gene turned back to Delta.

'It's a deal then. I'll go round the mob up and convince them you've gone,' he said. 'While I am doing that, you will be riding and you'll keep going. Savvy? Out of this province . . . gone.'

'Well, if the king pin says so, I suppose I've had worse offers,' Delta replied testily. He was losing the initiative but was prescient enough to see the obvious advantages. 'OK with you, Henry? Want to ride north with me?'

'Why not?' came the ready reply. 'We make a good team.'

'One last thing,' Bannerman warned. 'Wherever you wind up, Delta, keep away from my sister, understand? She is too good for the likes of you . . . it's bastards like you who have put her where she is today.'

Delta's eyes blazed.

'Why you mouthy bastard – listen to you! I've been looking out for Jordan on and off for years while you were off somewhere playing tin soldiers and telling the whole damn world what none-such wonder Texican you are. So don't give me any holier-than-thou sermons, Lancelot. I'll go, but I won't take that crap.'

Gene shoved him backwards. Hard. 'You'll stay away from my sister.'

'You're out of your mind. We ain't talking sweet little virgins here. Jordan's just a two-dollar whore for God's s—'

Bannerman's fist smashed into his mouth. Delta

staggered backwards, rebounded off the wall then retaliated with a pistoning right which knocked Bannerman off balance. As Delta swarmed in, Bannerman blocked with his forearms then head-butted to the jaw. Delta went loco. In an instant the two were locked together in a savage toe-to-toe which had Henry urging them on admiringly while the lawmen grabbed frantically at chairs to save them crashing over and attracting unwanted attention outside.

It was all too plain after a savage half-minute that Joe Delta and Gene Bannerman were too closely matched to achieve any result other than to beat one another into a pulp.

Neither quit first; it just ended, as though in mutual recognition of the fact that they couldn't continue. They stood facing with blood trickling from cuts and hammered noses, chests heaving and eyes flaring as the madness passed. It was just possible in those moments that, angry as they were, they were both realizing they had been less fighting each other than the fears and uncertainties confronting them both.

'I'll go out the front and you get out the back . . . and keep going north until you hit Texas,' Bannerman snarled, retrieving his hat.

'You bet I will. And if we don't see one another again it'll be a lifetime too soon.' Delta sleeved blood from his face. 'Ready to hightail, Henry boy?'

They were gone in moments.

Out on the square, Bannerman overcame the initial hostility of the mob by convincing them he'd cut all ties with Delta, and was now ready to help them search for him and see him swing for his crime. When they bought that he had little trouble in persuading them to join him in following up a 'lead' that someone had sighted their quarry skulking around the Amigo Horse Corrals on the north edge of town, looking for a mount to get him out of town, so it seemed.

A mile beyond the town limits, two men were riding beneath the stars, free and easy. But Delta wasn't making north as promised.

CHAPTER 9

STRIKEBACK

Joe Delta had a natural poker face.

The hardcase had been in so many brawls, gunfights, all-night poker games and complicated situations involving women, large sums of money and shifty-eyed men with knives up their sleeves, he'd learned young that the best method of handling the unexpected was to present a face devoid of all expression and wait for someone else to make the first move.

He knew they'd ridden around five miles to reach the battered little adobe hidden in a grove of pines south of town, but had no notion what the Rivera brothers and iron-faced Zeke Cromwell were doing seated there staring up at him and Henry, astonishment slowly fading as shock and anger took over.

As the seconds ticked by the brothers sat as though frozen. But the cattle king was coming up out of his chair with a face like thunder. Short, broad and ugly

as mortal sin, Cromwell radiated power and authority, was as two-fisted and dangerous as any man who
rode the giant ranch's forty-five thousand acres.

'By the power and glory, Henry, you'd better have
a good reason for—'

' 'Course I got good reason,' Henry interrupted,
cool and cocky as he moved round to rest his hands
on the backs of the Riveras' chairs. He nodded. 'Go
ahead, tell 'em, Joe. It's all over, ain't it?'

Delta was still as wary as an old dog in long grass-
snake country. 'Huh?'

'You and God A'mighty Bannerman, of course.'
Henry gestured. 'Just look at this joker's face, gents.
Pretty bad, huh? Well, Bannerman's looking twice as
bad.' He straightened and swaggered round the
room again. 'They've fallen out, might've shot it out
if I hadn't been there. They've busted up high, wide
and handsome. And the minute I got a whiff that Joe
here might be fixing to saddle up and head north,
why, I said to myself, "Dewey boy, is your outfit down
here doing so well that we can afford to just sit back
and watch one of the ringiest, two-gun hard men
we've ever laid eyes on just . . . go?" '

He made a flying motion with his arms, flowing
and graceful.

Suddenly they were catching on. The rancher's
hectic colour faded and the brothers finally leaned
back in their chairs some. They suspected everyone
but each other. They were playing a desperate game
here, their new ally their father's most dangerous
enemy. They needed some good news tonight.
Maybe – just maybe – this could be it. Cromwell

seemed to reckon so. 'Well, I be dogged.' The cattle baron almost managed a grin. 'What the man says true, boy?'

'Don't call me boy,' said Delta. Arched black brows lifted quizzically at Henry.

'Mebbe you better explain pronto – boy.'

If Henry trusted anything it was his own judgment. He'd had a flash of true inspiration a short time back and was ready to lay his cards on the table. He nodded to the scowling Delta.

'You're looking at Señor big-shot Rivera senior's worst enemies here, Joe boy. Zeke for obvious reasons, the boys on account they've been getting the short end of the stick from their old man all their lives and have finally had a bellyfull. Get the notion? And what are they doing together when they've been at war all their lives? Simple. After what's happened, they realized they could just throw in the towel and let Rivera go on tromping all over them, or – and this is bark with the bite in it – they could pard up, double their strength, and go for what all three of them crave. Namely, a tombstone for the *patrón*. So, they buried their grudges, shook hands, sat down to look at what needed to be done, and how, and of course, yours truly was put in charge of rounding up the extra gun talent they're gonna need. Only thing, I ended up inside, but that don't signify now I'm out. So, getting the picture now?'

Delta nodded. Maybe he was.

He glanced around. He sensed everyone was relaxing now, yet still kept his right hand close to gunbutt as he proceeded to draw out a chair with his toe and sat himself down. Taking out the makings, he studied each man in turn, their faces daubed a greasy yellow by the light of a single yellow candle rammed into the neck of a brown bottle. Dewey Henry coughed, then continued to broaden the picture for the benefit of all present.

Henry had been informed of the impending all-important final meeting between the Rivera boys and his boss Cromwell while behind bars, but had not expected to get to attend. Until Delta waltzed in to set him loose, that was.

He hastened to explain that it had never entered his mind to seek to enlist Delta's talents in what they called the 'operation', until he'd found himself forced to step back to avoid getting blood spattered all over him during the former partners' ferocious *calabozo* set-to.

Studying his bruised and battered features, the assembly appeared puzzled by this spectacular falling-out. Delta decided to explain.

'We were never pards,' he protested convincingly, lighting up. 'Bannerman was always too biggety and full of himself for mine, and now I'm sure as hell itchin' to square accounts when I see him next – the Sam Colt way.' He slapped a gun handle hard and Tomas Rivera twitched involuntarily. Two things the province already knew about Joe Delta had proven true that he was trouble, and deadly with the six guns.

'Matter of fact,' he went on, 'it was when my pard and yours, Henry here, seen how filthy I was on Bannerman that I guess he got sorta inspired.'

'Inspired?' a man said. 'How come?'

Delta leaned forward, expression intent. 'He sized up two things about me real quick. One, that I got it in for that uppity Rivera for reasons I ain't goin' into just now. But second and more important, *amigos*, after dishin' up your bunch out at the spread, Cromwell, I'm a big man on San Cristobal. And even though he ain't told me too much about you fellers and what you're about, Henry reckons I could play a mighty important part in making your operation a real success.'

Paulo Rivera proceeded to interrogate the new man. Delta's answers seemed to satisfy. When he got through, his brother and Cromwell traded long looks, finally both nodding togther. He was accepted, just as Henry tipped he would be.

It went swiftly from there. These were men in a hurry – a hurry to strike while the fires burned hot. In a hurry not to give themselves too much time to dwell on the magnitude of what they were undertaking, or what could befall all of them if they should fail. They kept glancing at Delta. He was plainly the ace in the hole they'd needed to fall into their laps in this high-stake game.

It lasted an hour. At the wind-up, hands were shaken, vows reaffirmed. Slumped in his chair, Delta didn't shake with anybody. He'd told them he was in; that was all they needed from him, he reasoned.

They broke out a bottle to toast their coming success and to welcome the new man into the pack. As part of his initiation, Delta sat sipping and listening as Dewey Henry painted a larger picture of Operation San Cristobal for his benefit, and some surprise. Ever since their father's return to Mexico with Matthew James years earlier, the brothers Rivera had been struggling to wrestle with that bolt from the blue. It seemed that having decreed both his sons incompetent, disloyal, greedy and obsessively secretive, the *patrón* had conceived and engineered the abduction of his illegitimate son in Texas with the express intention of making him his heir.

The brothers' resentment and bitterness had only deepened with time. But it had not been until quite recently that they had taken the giant step of deciding both father and stepbrother were expendable. But when they had sat down to draw up their plans for rebellion and dynasty change, they quickly realized they needed a powerful outside ally if they seriously hoped to ever take over glittering San Cristobal.

An alliance with Cromwell was a natural one. He hated Rivera as much as they did. Once organized, the brothers had helped plan and finance several Cromwell attacks on the ranch designed to weaken it and render it vulnerable to the ultimate attack.

The preamble to that final assault had been meant to be the ambush at Jiminez Basin, which may well have achieved its goal of bringing Rivera to his knees but for the intrusion of Bannerman and their mint new recruit, Joe Delta.

At this point all paused to stare at Delta, searching for any sign of surprise or repugnance at what he'd heard. They found none. Delta was smoking a cigarette and his marked-up face was blank. Tomas Rivera grunted almost admiringly. This was surely a genuine buckaroo whose assistance might prove invaluable, if they could just rely upon him. He was tough but temperamental.

Henry proceeded to bring Delta right up to the moment.

In the wake of the basin disaster, the brothers had gotten together with the decimated Cromwell crew to decide whether the campaign was all washed up or just getting under way.

They decided on the latter. With Zeke Cromwell's once lofty ambitions to become king of the province and replace his rival in the governor's chair now reduced to a simple obsession with vengeance, Paulo and Tomas had reassured him they would sooner be reduced to penniless outcasts than go on living under the shadow of the executioner's axe as repre-sented by father and stepbrother.

So the fresh battle plan was drawn up. And battle was the appropriate word. No guerrilla warfare or gradual chipping away at the Diego Rivera façade now. The plan was for the brothers to pull the nighthawks from Policarpo, the deep canyon which ran the five miles from the San Cristobal downtrail to the very *hacienda* itself.

Cromwell had seven able men left and could recruit two or three more. With the plotters' strength now greatly enhanced by the Henry–Delta combina-tion, they again represented a sizeable and formida-ble fighting force.

It was agreed it would be the brothers' task to nullify the home acre defences in any possible way, with specific emphasis on Cody Mears, the child's round-the-clock bodyguard.

The ultimate plan was to infiltrate the home acres and launch a full-blooded attack ... and let the leaves fall where they may.

Delta studied the Riveras. He himself was freely regarded as a Grade A son of a bitch, and it was almost pleasurable to realize there were people lower than he, in the case of Paulo and Tomas Rivera, one hell of a lot lower.

They were sitting here in their black suits and flat-brimmed hats calmly planning the deaths of their own parents – as calmly as though discussing the weather. It turned a man's guts – even his. But at least it showed how smart Diego Rivera had been to real-ize that his sons were just plain, stinking no-good, and then had taken steps to redeem the situation he found himself in.

Did Rivera love his child son? There was no telling. It scarcely added up as a loving family.

Then Henry was cutting in on what the brothers and Cromwell were discussing. Henry, tough and ambitious in his own right as Cromwell's *segundo*, had not as yet revealed the main reason behind his involv-ing Delta in tonight's grand plan. He'd seen the window of opportunity at the jailhouse, he stated, proceeded to spell it out for them all now.

'We need an inside man who's got guts and gunspeed,' he stated, his sideways glance at the brothers suggesting they had neither. 'That's my buddy, Joe. I see him shoe-horning his way into the ranch headquarters tonight and takin' out Cody Mears. We all agree he's the danger, that he's just gotta go. Sure, a risky job, even for a real slick gun like you, Joe boy. But what do you say, Zeke, boys? Seeing as success swings on cancelling Mears, I reckon that should rate a real big pay day, huh? I mean, by tomorrow you could be king pin, Zeke, while you boys will automatically get to be the most powerful buckaroos in the province of Portales.'

He paused. There were no objections. He was playing on their hungry dreams. He slapped his thigh.

'Mears dead, the San Cristobal defence automatically in tatters – almost too easy. And you, Joe, you get to play the key role, make a big name for yourself with Mears and even square accounts with Bannerman and knock his sneaky plans into a cocked hat. Everyone a winner!'

But if this were the case, why was Joe Delta, gunman, badman, rapist and hellion suddenly looking so uneasy now as a bottle was broached and the fine-tuning of the assault plan began in earnest?

Nobody knew, for nobody noticed.

Delta did not even know for sure himself what it was that was suddenly gnawing at his vitals, sending him grabbing hungrily for a glass of that raw red-eye.

But he soon would, and when it did it would surprise even him.

The night sky was vast and oversown with stars, the moon a golden hook in the south as San Cristobal slept, secure in its defences, its master and mistress reassured and serene as people should be when surrounded by wealth, possessions and the deadly guns and keen eyes of all those paid to protect them.

If there was any twinge of conscience threatening to deny Diego Rivera his good night's rest, it did not show as he dreamed on in the huge master bedroom. He had visited the boy's quarters before retiring to find him happy and calm as usual, despite the fact that this was Maria's night away in town. But Cody had been there, and Diego was always reassured by the fact that the gunman-bodyguard appeared almost as fond of Matthew James as his 'nanny'.

The customarily nocturnal Mears was at that moment fast asleep in his room down the hall from the boy's, door ajar, twin six gun belt hanging from his bedpost in easy reach. Yet he slept, and why not?

Cromwell had finally made his long-anticipated big play, and paid a fearful price. The brothers, of whom the gunman was constantly watchful and suspicious, were absent from headquarters as was often the case these days. Mears still nursed some private concerns, such as trying to figure why Bannerman and Delta should cause him such ongoing unease. But these were small everyday matters, and Cody Mears slept secure in the knowledge that sooner rather than later he would be rich enough to quit the gun trade before his best days had slipped before him, before some twenty-year-old kid with gunsmoke in his eyes got lucky and just blew him away.

The moon blazed down and the flung shadows of the hacienda looked like black pits where the night guards paced and the midnight wind stirred softly in the rambler roses. The distant thunder muttered like the Dark Gods' muffled laughter.

*

At last the whole town was quiet.

Cigar smoke trailed over Bannerman's shoulder as he made the long walk across the plaza below the lofted spire and cross of the old church and under the sleepy gaze of the pillar-box sentries at the governor's palace, who could now relax with the last would-be rioters finally off the streets.

The sentry tossed a salute at the passing American, knowing it had been him who had poured the oil over troubled waters that night. Gene acknowledged with a flick of the cigar, bootheels sucking in the dust as he approached the filligreed wrought-iron façade of the ancient hotel.

This was one weary Texan, played out from anger, from effort, from the effects of iron-hard fists belting him from one side of the old *calabozo* to the other. His knuckles were skinned, his eyes were gritty and all he could think of was ten hours sleep.

Yet nonetheless, he was feeling chipper enough as he mounted the steps. For the way in which events had played out tonight, he might easily have had his true mission to Mexico exposed. In which case he could well be either dead or hightailing for the Rio empty-handed right this minute.

That disaster had been averted for the time being at least, and that alone was cause enough for him to feel positive as he pushed his way through the hotel's scarred front doors into the lobby.

Positive, but in no way complacent.

Plainly Delta hadn't yet blown the whistle on him. But that gunner was now very much a loose cannon and could go off unexpectedly any moment. There

135

was no way of being sure he'd headed for home; he could be sore enough to be spilling his guts about himself and his quest for the kid right at this minute to anyone who cared listen. He mightn't have much time.

But the rest had to be number one priority. He was counting on a full night's sleep to set him up with the clear head he would need in the morning to plot, implement and carry off the trick of ripping the kid free of the Riveras and making it to the border. Like, real fast.

He felt he could fall asleep still walking.

'Gene.'

He whirled. 'Maria! What. . . ?'

She rose from the lobby sofa and came forwards, her face tired and strained. She had been concerned about him, she told him. Had needed to wait and ensure he had survived the wild night safely before returning to the ranch.

He was impressed, and it seemed the most natural thing for him to take her hands in his and squeeze hard in appreciation. Their eyes met and held and he was aware of something stealing over him, something powerful and unexpected which he could not quite explain, which took him unawares.

'Everything is just fine,' he insisted. 'Come on, I'll walk you to the livery. Hope your driver was able to grab some shut-eye.' He was reluctant to see her go, the more so because he knew only too well that, after tomorrow, Maria Gonzales would spit at the very mention of his name if his plans played out. If not, in all probability, she would get to spit on his grave.

'Goodnight,' he smiled, as the driver drew a blanket over her knees and gathered up the reins. He touched her hand and suddenly she leaned down and kissed his cheek. There was no doubt about it, he realized, stepping back with one hand to his face, watching them go. This was undeniably his biggest day since crossing the border. Maybe ever. He could only hope it would not also prove to be his last.

Two horsemen rode beside the river.

'You've gone quiet, pard. Not havin' second thoughts are you?'

Riding at Dewey Henry's side where the trail clung to the river bank, Delta made no reply for the good reason he didn't hear.

Right at that moment he was travelling the strange trails of the mind. His thoughts had been sinking deeper and darker ever since they'd set out for the big ranch, taking him off to strange places, forcing Joe Delta to look at things about himself and his hell-for-leather life in a way he'd never done before.

He should be riding high. He'd beat up Bannerman, cut adrift of the pain-in-the-ass 'crusader' and signed on for a gun job worth one thousand dollars, US. If that wasn't what you called a solid night's work he didn't know what was. So why the mood? What did he care about any dumb kid, even if it was Jordan's? This lousy country had more kids than it could feed – and, besides, he needed a grubstake to get him back to Santa Fe or maybe Dodge.

Was he worried about Mears? He snorted aloud at

137

the notion. He feared nobody. He supposed Bannerman had to be the hardest man he'd ever faced and he knew he'd bested him, even if that big bastard didn't know it himself. So Mears was chain lightning and never slept, so they claimed. So?

'Joe?'

'Huh?'

'You're mighty quiet.'

'Sure, guess so. You ain't, though.'

Henry's teeth flashed whitely as he raised his face to the sky. He'd been all talk and high spirits since they'd quit the main bunch to head in for the hacienda.

In many ways he was a Delta soul brother in so far as both mostly lived for the day, for the excitement, the danger and the lure of big money. Despite the fact that he was Cromwell's right bower and the most formidable guntipper the plotters possessed, he would still be locked up fast in the town jug but for Delta's chance intervention. Could have missed the Big One altogether for no better reason than he'd gotten drunk and disorderly. But now he was bright, eager and just rearing to go as he shaped up to what might well prove be the biggest night of his life. Delta almost envied him.

'I've just got this big feelin' that everythin's come together fast tonight, and it's coming' together right, Joe. That's how I like it. Zeke's dead eager and the Riveras are primed to go all the way at last, and we got a good bunch of hard men backing us. Now all we got to do is—'

'What happens to the kid?'

138

'Huh?'

'I take Mears out, the boys pour in from the canyon and with luck it'll be all over in minutes,' Delta growled. 'But nobody said what happens to the kid?'

Henry studied him narrowly. 'You're kidding, right? I mean, what's a kid? We're fixing the biggest showdown this neck of the woods ever seen, and you're talking about some dumb kid?'

That was exactly how it seemed to Dewey Henry. But he was not a friend of years' standing of the child's mother. Had not promised he'd stick with Bannerman and run every mother-loving risk in the book if necessary to rescue her son before he forgot he ever had a real mother named Terasina Jordan.

It sounded anything but crazy to Joe Delta now his temper had cooled and he'd had time to slot his resentment towards Bannerman into perspective. This left him free to take a fresh look at the sudden offer of big dollars and gun glory as opposed to a promise made and a sentiment never seriously considered before, much less seen as some fulcrum upon which his scapegrace life might now swing.

An image jumped into his mind: a laughing young dark-eyed woman holding a baby on her shoulder against the backdrop of the sunlit Rio Grande.

Another picture: the kid coming across the patio hand in hand with his nanny at the ranch, seeming to be focused directly upon Delta, a stranger now.

Another: the smouldering ruins of the greatest *casa* in the region and a small body in the rubble – this image superimposed over another of a woman weeping forever – maybe all because of wild Joe Delta.

He reined in abruptly where the trail curved sharply round a stand of cottonwoods.

'What?' Henry said sharply. He was all fired up for action, and the other's odd mood was beginning to rile him.

'Change of plans. I'm not going to do it. I'm heading back to town.' He shrugged. 'What you could call a change of heart. I'm going back to get drunk.'

Henry paled. 'This some kind of joke, buddy?'

'Straight A.'

'That doesn't suit, Joe.' Something had happened to Henry's clean-cut face. His eyes appeared smoky when he flashed a savage grin as he rested hand on gunbutt and allowed his mount to ease off a ways. 'Nobody welches this far into the deal with yours truly. We made a deal. We're in this together and that's how it's gotta be.'

'Sorry.'

'You mean. . . ?'

Henry's voice faded. He'd been about to challenge the other if he was ready to back his stand with iron. But Delta's cold grey eyes and his too-still posture in the saddle handed him the answer with cold-deck certainty.

Henry saw red.

His draw was smooth and very fast, the Colt leaping eagerly from its holster with thumb curving the hammer back as it flashed upwards.

Delta was faster.

He came clear and triggered in an effortless unhurried motion. For a timeless moment, Henry

140

thought the shot had missed. Then he felt the
massive agony explode in his chest, and the crimson
soak his shirt. Before the astonished look faded from
his face, Delta killed him with a bullet through the
throat that cut his windpipe and shattered his back-
bone.

Delta refilled his smoking gun with steady fingers.
His face was stone. He kicked the animal into a run
and was gone before the ranch rig carrying Maria
Gonzales appeared through the cottonwoods in the
moonlight.

One hour later, Gene Bannerman walked warily
across the bend in the trail where Dewey Henry lay
stark beneath the moon. He struck another match
and peered at the ground as Maria and the driver
watched in frozen silence. It had taken the shocked
girl some time to rush back to Morelos and alert the
tall Texan of their grisly find, then return. She was
hoping Bannerman might uncover some explana-
tion for the killing other than that it could be somehow connected to the spread, as she feared might be
the case.

No such luck.

When Gene finally found a clear set of prints of
the killer's horse he recognized them at a glance.
Delta's buckskin. And he was heading directly for
San Cristobal. A cold hand touched his heart. Until
that moment it hadn't occurred to him that Delta
might swing against him, even if he didn't quit the
province. But Henry's bullet-shattered corpse and
that set of prints running east created a manuscript

of the night all too easy to read.

Should Delta be on his way to Rivera to apprise him of the real reason behind their presence in the province, then any slim chance Bannerman may have had of recovering his nephew would be zero. But what could Delta hope to gain? Apart from revenge and possibly reward, that was. He grimaced. More than enough incentive for that bastard. He would inform on his own mother for less.

He realized the girl was at his side, eyes searching his face. She seemed to understand him as few others ever had. And staring failure and a potential tragedy in the making as the iron moments ground by, he made the only decision that made sense. If Delta had spilled his guts to Rivera, as appeared certain, then the doors of San Cristobal would be closed to him. Rescuing Matthew James would be impossible once the alarm was raised. But if Maria truly loved the child as he suspected was the case, then she might help him yet – if she knew exactly who and what he was. What did he have to lose?

So he told her everything.

Her response was to slip her hand into his and tearfully reveal her own secret. She had long wanted to spirit the child away from the tensions, the undercurrents and the threatening atmosphere of that divided family, yet had found the task far beyond her. But his stunning revelations were like a blessing, she wept. But were they too late? What was happening tonight? Was this to be the doomsday she had long felt hanging over the ruthless Rivera and his sinister, scheming sons? For wasn't that an old Aztec blood moon above – portend of doom?

But for Bannerman it was abruptly time for decision, not questions. He was soon breaking trail for the ranch astride his blaze-faced black, fighting fear every mile. Not fear for himself but for his sister's child.

CHAPTER 10

TEXAS CAMELOT

The gold clock on the marble mantelpiece ticked towards four. The match in Diego Rivera's hand was unsteady. He lit the cheroot, flicked the vesta into the gleaming cuspidor near his boots.

'Trouble, you say, Señor Delta?' he rasped, irritable at having been dragged out of bed at such a ridiculous hour for so seemingly nebulous a reason. 'You say you anticipate trouble here tonight, you are uncertain what kind, yet you considered it important enough to awaken the entire headquarters?'

It was true. San Cristobal was wide awake in the darkest hour before dawn. Lights blazed, nighthawks prowled the surrounds clutching carbines. The cook was even brewing coffee in the galley. And all because the Americano had arrived at the gates with his evil news, leaving the nightwatch no option but to awaken the *patrón* and disturb the whole compound in the process.

Now, for their troubles, it seemed Rivera might be in the mood to start firing people any moment as he awaited his answer.

'Rustlers,' grunted Delta, checking out the magnificent clock. He looked back over his shoulder showing a face that looked like it had been worked over by a stave. Yet he was cool. The ice man, seemingly unaware of the disturbance he was creating here in the pre-dawn chill. He nodded. 'Yessir, chanced to pick up on some snatches of booze talk at the Piedra Cantina tonight. Enough to convince me a big bunch of cow thieves are gonna hit your prime herds sometime tonight.'

He cut his gaze to the third man in the room. '*Sabe?*'

Cody Mears stood before an intricately carved bookcase with arms folded and head tilted back. The sleek bodyguard was fully dressed right down to his guns. His face was unreadable as he studied the nightcomer, yet Delta felt a weakening run through him as their glances locked. Mears was surely the genuine article. You could always tell the breed. Fast, cold and deadly. And this was the man he would have to kill sometime before first light – no matter which way this night played out. Best of luck, Joe boy.

'Where is Bannerman?' Mears wanted to know.

'Tuckered out. Turned in early. So I elected to ride out alone.'

Mears glanced at his employer. 'He's lyin''. *Teniente* Orlando told Creed this bum and Bannerman had a brawl at the jailhouse, damned near killed one another.'

Rivera's face darkened ominously as he approached Delta.

'You lie to us? You dare? And for what reason? You will confess or by the Virgin you will be dealt with like any other dog who betrays our hospitality.'

At that moment the doña, large and rumpled in a vast cerise nightcoat, poked her bonneted head around the corner, demanding querulously to know what was going on.

Delta took the opportunity to light a cigarette he really needed, shot another swift glance at the fat clock as it chimed the hour.

Where were they?

The brothers' plan was to strike the hacienda before first light. Maybe the bunch was hanging back out in the canyon when they'd heard no gunfire from the hacienda. The plan was for Delta to use his association with Rivera to get into the headquarters and then take out the feared Mears before they launched the full attack. That would have to mean gunshots.

Or maybe something else had delayed them, he mused. Maybe something that might have even caused them to turn back?

He shook his head at the thought. Sweat trickled down his spine.

Joe Delta, the hardcase gun who liked to brag he had no nerves, was tonight riding a lethal rollercoaster that could easily see him dead six times over before he could jump off.

And outside someplace, Cromwell and the brothers and their gun-toting dog pack were waiting for him to play his part, sworn to kill him if he let them down. Here, people who likely despised him and only let him near the place on account of Bannerman – watching like hawks, suspicious, the *patrón* hostile, every man ready to his every order, instantly.

And Mears.

He cursed viciously beneath his breath as the weighed seconds ticked by. Where the hell were they?

He'd made his way right into the lion's den in order to be right on hand to take out Mears. The plan was for him to do that the moment the main party launched their attack after coming up from the canyon to the casa via the zoo, when the first volley rocked the hacienda and diverted the gunman.

Maybe he'd better get his ass out of this high-ceilinged barn of a room with its vivid Mexican tapestries and bristling guns, with Mears looking proddier by the minute. Find out what was delaying the bunch. Put his own secret plan on hold. . . .

He flicked his butt into the grate and hitched at his gunbelt. He was a picture of hardcase confidence hitched at his gunbelt and headed casually towards those tall double doors.

'Señor Rivera, Mears, what say I go take a look—'

'Something stinks here, boss,' Mears cut in

sharply, crossing the room with leopard grace. 'He's playing some game and lyin' about it. Give me five minutes with the sonuva and we'll either know what he's up to or he won't be around to worry us about him any.'

'As you wish,' Rivera replied without hesitation. 'But make sure the boy is properly guarded first.'

'Now just a blamed minute,' protested Delta. But it was already too late for talk. In one dazzling blur of motion, Mears whipped out a .45 and shoved the muzzle up against the Texan's bruised jaw. 'Shuck the irons and get your dirty hands behind your head, small-time. Now!'

Delta was raging inside. He couldn't believe he'd been bested so easily. The vaunted guntipper had him ice cold. With no option, he was reaching for his gunbelt and bracing himself for the worst when the sound of running feet came from the patio and a wide-eyed house servant rushed stumbling into the great room.

'*Patrón*,' he panted. 'Maria has returned from Morelos . . . and Señor Bannerman is with her. The *señor*, like Señor Delta, now also wishes to see you, *patrón*.'

'*Madre de Dios*!' exploded Rivera. 'Has the world gone mad? All right, all right, show the *gringo* in. But, Cody, stay by me. There is something rotten abroad this night and I fear for . . . I know not what it is I fear.'

'I understand, *patrón*,' said Mears. He turned to the servants. 'Well, you heard. Bring them in.' And cocked his .45 as he backed away from Delta to take his place at his master's side, where he belonged.

Bannerman strode into the room moments later trailed by the girl with the blue-black hair. Rivera scowled in total confusion while Delta, the loser, grinned cynically at the manner in which his big night, so carefully planned to be so very different, seemed to be collapsing into chaos before his eyes.

Yet in the heat of the moment, Mears had made an error. For Joe Delta still had his guns.

But nobody noticed, for Gene Bannerman and Maria had entered just at the climactic moment to join the other principals in the drama, the whole scene momentarily frozen beneath the glare of the lights – while the larger drama was unfolding offstage.

This was before Delta dared make a play; before Cody Mears could quieten his instincts that warned of danger; before *Patrón* Rivera could understand why in hell the peace of his hacienda's night was being rudely shattered. It was even before Maria could breathe one quick prayer for no violence – that a frightening sound trembled the candelabra and the chandeliers like a voice out of hell.

Magnified in the chill night air and as primitive as the deepest jungle, the tiger's angry roar raised neck hairs and set spines tingling for long seconds which felt more like minutes, to be suddenly engulfed by the bellow of a rifle and a man's death scream of agony coming from the direction of the zoo.

Joe Delta was first to respond, for only he knew

now that fifteen gunmen had successfully traversed Jiminez Canyon to reach the hacienda proper – the Rivera heartland.

He was gone in the blink of an eye.

Mears made to give chase but Rivera's shout saw the gunman instead pivot and follow the *patrón* for the rear patio, both men bawling orders as, a hundred yards away, tousle-headed cowboys and wranglers tumbled out the doors of the long adobe bunkhouses, fumbling with their weapons as they prepared to confront whatever threatened the governor's hacienda.

The mansion was rocking to the first thunderous volleys as Bannerman and Maria, two people with but a single thought, sped down the green-carpeted passageway for Matthew James's nursery.

Gene had no notion who might be attacking, only knew that the diversion was a miracle of timing which was offering them some slim chance to achieve what they'd set out to do, before the headquarters went totally crazy.

There was no way of knowing what madness was erupting over in the zoo sector, which Rivera himself had so proudly shown him over before, other than it was beginning to sound like Bull Run all over now as bullets smashed into stucco, adobe, glass and tile and the night rocked to the voices and howling of men locked in savage battle.

'Gene! Look!'

Maria's cry took him to a window. His jaw muscles locked. Beyond an archway giving on to the huge walled inner garden of the great hacienda where a

150

lamplit fountain burbled musically, where shouting figures were rushing this way and that, he had his first clear glimpse of the invaders in the shape of Tomas Rivera and several Cromwell riders bursting their way through a canvas-roofed annexe that gave on to the horseyards.

They were shooting off in the direction of the central room.

Maria bit her hand to stifle an involuntary scream, but it broke loose anyway. He seized her by the arm to drag her away from the spectacle. Their movement attracted attention of the wrong kind when an ugly thug of a raider, big-shouldered, bearded and wielding a repeater rifle, came lunging through from a flanking portico, bristling with excitement and hate, ready to kill.

'Death to Rivera, the great tyrant!' he roared the split-second before Bannerman fanned six gun hammer to drive two bullets through his wide-open mouth and blew out the back of his skull.

The man fell like a butchered beef.

Bannerman didn't spare him a glance. The night was gripped by madness and it was plainly, chillingly, a case of fight or die.

And maybe some of the madness affected him now as, realizing Maria had half-swooned, succumbing to hysteria, he stepped over her legs where she'd collapsed on the Persian carpet and with both big black guns roaring defiantly, went out to meet the invaders of Rivera's castle face to face.

He was heavily outnumbered.

But the blinding action that followed proved the

enemy to be no more than mere journeymen of the gun plying their plodding trade, the tall Texan a knight errant fighting for a cause, and might was his right.

Scythed off their feet by whistling lead, they tumbled like ninepins, hazed by evil veils of gunsmoke, men he'd never seen before, faceless men dying for glory or money, he didn't know which, but dying fast and hard.

A bullet burned his upper arm. He ducked low and triggered a charging dark-garbed figure astride a gleaming red stallion. At close range the bullet tore a hole in the man as big as a fist where it exploded out his back. The horse veered away and the centre-shot body of Paulo Rivera smashed to the pavement, head-first and dead.

The attackers had fallen back, giving him a chance to back up some. He was panting hard and shaking his head when a sudden movement off to the right where the curving gallery of the north wing reached away, caught his eye.

For a moment, the tall figure slipping and sliding on spilled blood on marbled floors was just a silhouette. Then the man moved into a bar of light spilling from the library doors, and he could clearly see the man – and the terrified child he was dragging behind him one-handed.

Delta and Matthew James! The bastard!

For a moment he was stunned. But for no longer. His right hand gun sprouting from his fist, he whispered a prayer to the god of straight-shooting, was depressing trigger as Delta's wild shout reached his ears.

'No, Bannerman, it's not what you think, you—'

The roar of the shot momentarily blotted out the bedlam of noises, rocking the Rivera hacienda. Instantly Joe Delta was punched away from the child, slammed into a huge window and vanished.

Next instant the child was running towards him.

Bannerman didn't remember rushing forward to sweep up the small figure in his arms. He whirled to see Maria come through the archway, before smacking into a statue of some Andalusian saint and smashing it as though hit by a sledgehammer. The child screamed. Who could blame him?

Then, 'This way, Gene. Hurry, *por favor.*'

Holding up her skirts, slippered feet flashing, Maria led him down a shadowy passageway which he sensed was taking them away from the danger zone. The hacienda was enormous. They seemed to run forever, taking corners, up one corridor and down another – but it could have only been a half-minute before the girl flung open a set of a double doors and Gene recognized the wide downsweep of carefully tended lawns and gardens spreading before him in the moonlight. They'd reached the front of the mansion where they'd left the buggy and horses – and now the roar of the battle sounded muffled and distant.

He wanted to kiss her but there was no time for that. Holding the sobbing child tightly against his chest, he followed the girl across the patio and down moonlit steps, and was just breaking into full stride when he heard her choked-off gasp.

He stopped on a dime as the slender figure

emerged from the heavy black moonshadows where the horses waited.

Wordlessly he handed Matthew James to Maria.

Mears stood empty-handed, his face a taut mask of supreme arrogance and icy triumph as he halted and spread his boots.

'Hero of the gun,' he said with soft malevolence. 'The reader and the quoter. But too damn dumb to do anything other than the bloody obvious.' His expression changed. 'You're going to die for this, Texan. This kid is my responsibility . . . and you are a lying, treacherous, double-crossing son of a bitch. Draw!'

Bannerman went into the draw. There was no option. He knew he'd never been faster, never surer. Yet he didn't even get a shot away before the gun that had filled Mears' fist as though by sleight of hand blossomed orange and wicked and a great blow struck his shoulder and sent him reeling as the blast of the .45 rolled over him.

The child screamed as he was falling. Another shot thundered yet he felt nothing. Mears was walking towards him through the smoke, firing as he came, yet his bullets were well wide of the intended target, ripping great gouges in the fine grass on either side of him.

He was playing with him!

Gene's gun was gone. Left-handed he clawed for the other and saw his death in the gunman's eyes as he loomed above him. Mears extended his gun arm and the muzzle was huge in Bannerman's eyes. He saw finger whiten on trigger, heard the shot, again felt nothing.

Mears was reeling away like a drunk, an odd sound coming from his throat.

Bannerman jerked his head round as a familiar figure came staggering down the wide steps. Bracing himself with a herculean effort, an ashen Cody Mears was trying to work his piece when Delta's gun stormed again with judgment day authority. Mears dropped to one knee and tried desperately to lift his gun. But the weapon weighed a ton and all he could do was stare up at the approaching figure with a face alive with inhuman hate in the final seconds of life before Joe Delta shot him between the eyes.

The smoking gun swung on Bannerman.

'I ought to give you one – blasting me, Bannerman.' Delta looked bad but his voice was strong. 'I was taking the kid away, damn you. You ain't the only true-blue hero in the business, even if you think you are.'

'But . . . but you killed that man on the trail . . . and you were riding with that bunch. . . .'

'Why don't you start preaching?' Delta's voice was rough, almost savage. Then he jerked around at the rising sound of shooting from the mansion. 'Or maybe that will have to wait. Come on, it's a long way to the Rio Grande!'

Bannerman allowed Maria to assist him to his feet. He hurt like hell but was starting to grin. They were on the trail in moments with the sounds of violence swiftly fading behind. And Delta was right. It was a long way to the Rio. Yet despite the bullet lodged in his side, his former or current enemy or partner – take your pick – drove every mile.

'Nice evening, Gene.'

'Mighty fine, Garve.'

Gunsmith Garve Wilson was new leader of the Family of Friends. Bannerman had quit on his return from Mexico and everyone seemed to understand why. Now he was just another regular citizen strolling homewards through the streets of Keylock where nothing seemed to have changed, and there was no reason why it should.

It was months since their return to Texas had been closely followed by the news from Mexico of the destruction of the Rivera family and the razing of San Cristobal. Many weeks had passed since Jordan had agreed to come live with him, and just as long since she had taken a drink. Since Matthew James had begged good friends Maria and Joe to join them, and for two people who loved him, an offer impossible to refuse.

The months and weeks which had seen blazing summer give way to blizzard-breath mid-winter, the richest season of Bannerman's thirty-seven years.

He rounded the final corner and Maria and the boy were there on the front steps of the big house, all muffled-up and smiling, waiting for him. Matthew James broke loose of Maria's gloved hand and came running towards him, his cries bringing Jordan and Delta out on to the gallery, hand in hand.

It was just like Camelot, Gene Bannerman mused

as he knelt to hug the boy and looked up to see the look in his wife's green eyes. Except this was all real. As real as the poet's words:

'The Grail exists in the hearts of brave men. They find it through great deeds and are content.'